"I Know The Way," Jessie Insisted.

"But I give door-to-door service," Ben said. "You'll thank me for this."

He helped her out of the car, then put his arm around her waist as if it belonged there. Ben took her house key from her hand, opened her front door and glanced around inside. Then he returned the key with a kiss.

His touch was rough, hungry. Her heart leapt in response to his lips. Then he slowly pulled away.

"What am I thanking you for?" she asked.

Ben shook his head slightly. "This time, I was thanking you."

"How do I tell the difference?"

"Practice," he said, whispering into the night air.

Dear Reader,

June is a terrific month. It's the time of year when the thoughts of women—and men—turn to love . . . *and* marriage. Not only does June mark the beginning of those hot, lazy days of summer, it's also a month with a fantastic, fiery lineup from Silhouette Desire.

First, don't miss the sizzling, sensational *Man of the Month, The Goodbye Child* by Ann Major, which is the latest in her popular Children of Destiny series. Also in June, look for *The Best Is Yet To Come,* another story of blazing passion and timeless romance from the talented pen of Diana Palmer.

Rounding out June are four other red-hot stories that are sure to kindle your emotions written by favorite authors Carole Buck, Janet Bieber and—making their Silhouette Desire debuts—Andrea Edwards and Amanda Stevens.

So get out those fans and cool down . . . then heat up with stories of sensuous, emotional love—only from Silhouette Desire!

All the best,

Lucia Macro
Senior Editor

ANDREA EDWARDS

STARTING OVER

Published by Silhouette Books New York

America's Publisher of Contemporary Romance

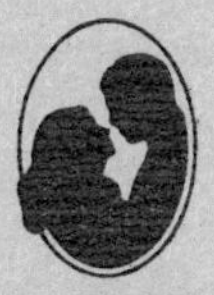

SILHOUETTE BOOKS
300 East 42nd St., New York, N.Y. 10017

STARTING OVER

ISBN: 0-373-05645-1

First Silhouette Books printing June 1991

Printed in the U.S.A.

Books by Andrea Edwards

Silhouette Special Edition

Rose in Bloom #363
Say It with Flowers #428
Ghost of a Chance #490
Violets Are Blue #550
Places in the Heart #591
Make Room for Daddy #618

Silhouette Intimate Moments

Above Suspicion #291

Silhouette Desire

Starting Over #645

ANDREA EDWARDS

is the pseudonym of Anne and Ed Kolaczyk, a husband-and-wife writing team that concentrates on women's fiction. "Andrea" is a former elementary school teacher, while "Edwards" is a refugee from corporate America, having spent almost twenty-five years selling computers before becoming a full-time writer. They have four children, two dogs and four cats, and live in South Bend, Indiana.

To Joanne,
who was the height of understanding
when deadlines came close.

One

The downpour had subsided to a drizzle—slow, steady and a bit on the cool side for June—but for once Jessie didn't mind that she had left her umbrella in the hall at home. She needed something to dampen her anger before she exploded.

That man was impossible! How could the city hire him to head the juvenile division of the police department? He was thickheaded, stubborn and so damn sure of himself she wanted to scream.

Jessie hurried down the steps of the police station, her hands tightening into fists of frustration no matter how she tried to will them to relax. In her eight years as a social worker, she'd had to deal with all sorts of people, from unsympathetic teachers to incompetent bureaucrats, but ten minutes with Captain Benjamin Adamanti and she was ready to commit mayhem.

Turning to squeeze herself between two parked cars, Jessie tried to keep her raincoat from brushing against either car and took a deep breath. Everybody in the office had warned her about him, but the thing she'd remembered best was Marla saying what a hunk the guy was. As if Jessie cared! Having hit the big three-oh this year, she was a bit beyond the giggly stage of falling in love with every blue-eyed man. And why did she remember Ben Adamanti had blue eyes? a little voice asked.

Jessie's only response was to quicken her pace as she jammed her hand into her coat pocket, letting her fingers search for her car keys. All they found was an old gum wrapper. Oh, no! Not again.

She stopped in the middle of an aisle, right behind her car, and tried her other pocket. A tissue and a lucky penny she'd found in the parking lot on her way in. Damn. Some luck it had brought her.

Feeling as if a pit of quicksand were swallowing her up, she trudged the few remaining steps to her car. Her hand was rummaging her purse, but she knew it was useless. And she was right. There, dangling from the ignition, were her keys. While here, on the other side of a locked door, was she. Frustration moved her to do the only thing any reasonable, sane person would—she kicked one of the tires.

"Having trouble, Miss Taylor?"

Jessie spun at the sound of the smooth voice. It couldn't be. Damn. It was. The six-foot-two-inch hunk she'd just battled with. "Hello, Captain."

"Ben," he said, and finished walking over to the car. "Something wrong here?"

Admitting she locked her keys in the car would make her sound flighty, stupid, irresponsible, and yet she couldn't exactly pretend all was fine. "Nothing much," she said. "Just getting a little tension out of my system. You're wrong about Robbie, you know. He didn't mean anybody any harm."

Ben sighed, looking like he, too, was edging close to mayhem. "That kid you're defending stole more than three hundred dollars worth of tapes and CDs. Besides, I thought we covered all this just a few minutes ago."

"Not to my satisfaction."

"The kid belongs in detention."

"He belongs where he'll get some help." Continuing their argument wasn't what she wanted. Getting a coat hanger to unlock her car was. But without Ben Adamanti as a witness. "What did you do, follow me out here so we could keep on arguing?" She leaned against the car next to hers, arms folded across her chest and, hopefully, a look of suspicion and accusation across her face.

"Hardly. That's my car you're leaning against. I was just on my way to lunch when I saw you trying to punt your car."

"Oh. Well, excuse me." She moved away from his car, waving her hand at it to indicate he was free to go. "I certainly wouldn't want to impede the progress of the law."

But he didn't take her up on her offer and rush into his car. Rather, he stood there watching her, suspicion narrowing his eyes. Doggone it, now what?

"It's raining," he said.

"Not much anymore. Feels kind of nice." She smiled up at the sky as if letting the drizzle frizz up her short brown hair was her favorite pastime. "There's nothing like a gentle rain in June to cleanse the air and the soul."

Captain Adamanti didn't look fooled. The line of his jaw said he didn't give in, he didn't compromise. He wasn't going to drive off and leave her here.

Ben Adamanti was everything she disliked in a man. Tall, dark and husky—all right, so that wasn't his fault. Nevertheless, his rock-hard stance on everything was hardly genetic. She liked a man who was sensitive, willing to talk things out and compromise, one who wouldn't make her feel like an incompetent fool for locking her keys in her car. But maybe she was wrong about him.

She paused a moment to try to read the policeman's eyes. Obstinacy, suspicion and impatience. Not a very encouraging assortment. Her gaze darted away, and her mind drifted back to his office, trying to remember if there had been some clue to a softer side to his nature. Although, no matter how hard she tried, not a single personal item came to mind. She thought of the little cartoon on her wall about a neat desk being the sign of a sick mind. A neat office had to be even worse. Maybe she could drive him away by returning to their argument.

"I think that theft was just Robbie's way of crying out for help," Jessie told him. The suspicion in his eyes turned to impatience. Just leave if you don't want to hear this again, she silently told him. I won't be offended. "I know Robbie. His parents went through a bitter divorce a few years back and he hardly saw his father. But then this past fall, his father died and he's having a hard time dealing with it."

"It doesn't mean he can break the law." The man leaned against his car instead of getting into it.

Jessie jammed her hands into her pockets. Was it her imagination or had the rain started to come down a bit harder? "No, but Robbie's doing so doesn't mean that he's a criminal. All I was asking for was probation and counseling."

"That's for a judge to decide."

Didn't the guy have any compassion? Her eyes flashed down to his hands. No wedding ring. Did that mean no kids, either?

"Hey, we both know that you can ask for a plea and get it," Jessie said. "All I ask is that you don't throw the book at him just yet."

Captain Adamanti straightened up, seeming to fill up the small space between the cars with his broad shoulders. Jessie held her ground as he walked past her, refusing to move because of the light brushing of his arm as he walked by. His after-shave had a woodsy scent to it, sending her just the tiniest whiff of it as he passed. It made her think of camp fires and tents, of sleeping bags and bodies huddled together to ward off the cold, of—

"All right," he said.

Jessie started, fire blazing her cheeks in response to the direction of her thoughts. No, he hadn't been able to read them. That had never been one of the talents mentioned in the newspaper articles about him when he'd come here to South Bend.

"You'll ask for probation?"

He stopped at the rear of her car. "I'll ask the court to order a psychological and emotional evaluation," he said. "If they agree with what you're saying, I'll go for probation."

She wanted to hug the man, but it was a fleeting thought—very fleeting. Or was it? The look on his face certainly didn't invite hugs, even hugs of relief and excitement, yet there was a primitive urge down deep in her soul that was trying to push her closer to him. It wasn't an urge she wanted to explore, and certainly not one she intended to act on.

"Thank you so much," she said with careful courtesy.

He said nothing, just stood there staring at her. Making her nervous. She licked her lips.

"Then you'll have Robbie sent to the Family Center until the evaluation is done?"

"Yes, Miss Taylor," he said. "Don't worry. I'm not going to secretly sneak him off to prison."

"I hardly thought you would," she said. Why didn't he leave? Embarrassment, relief and some other undercurrents she couldn't quite name all churned together in her stomach. "I mean, no matter what else, I believe you're a man of your word."

"No matter what else?" he echoed.

Lord, where was her sense? "I meant, that even though we might not agree on everything, I do trust you."

"Thank you, I think." His voice seemed to hold a trace of laughter, as if he were mocking her, but his eyes were still as hard and distant as ever, so she wasn't certain.

"Well, we'd both better be going," she said, and took a step closer to her car door, as if she were about to start looking for her keys.

"Oh, Miss Taylor." His voice stopped her.

"Yes?"

"Do you want some help getting your car unlocked?"

He was laughing at her, no doubt about it now. She turned slowly to face him. His eyes were glittering with laughter. He probably thought she had no brains, that she was a real airhead.

"I guess I was so worried about Robbie that I was a little careless. I've never done this before." At least not here in the police station parking lot, she quickly added so it wasn't technically a lie.

"Want me to call someone to help you? It's lunchtime, but I'm sure there are some mechanics hanging around in the city garage there."

"No." She shook her head. "I'll just get a hanger from the coatrack inside."

His eyebrows raised. "I thought you've never done this before."

"I've seen it done," she said. When he didn't respond, she blew up. "All right, so I've done it before. Now, will you go so I can get my car open in peace?"

"And be accused of leaving a lady in distress?"

She didn't need his mockery, or the wretched embarrassment of feeling like a fool. "Look, I don't believe in knights in shining armor. I slay all my own dragons. And open my own doors, including this one."

"I'll drive you back up to the door for your hanger," he offered.

But she refused to move. "If you don't mind . . ."

"I'm gone," he said. The laughter in his eyes had disappeared, and soon so was he.

She was glad, Jessie told herself as she trudged back to the station all by herself. Although her heart refused to join the celebration. She'd been rude and there was no excuse for it. It was hardly Ben Adamanti's fault that she'd learned at an early age that fairy tales don't come true. That the one thing she couldn't stand was being laughed at.

Jessie forced a smile onto her face as she went back inside. Well, at least she'd won a reprieve for Robbie. So why wasn't her heart singing a little tune of joy?

A frown of determination wrinkled her brow. It would. Real quick. Just as soon as the scent of that after-shave left the air.

"So how'd the meeting go?" Marla asked when Jessie came back to the office.

"Don't ask." Jessie threw her purse onto her desk. Her car keys followed.

"That bad, huh?" Marla swung her cowboy-booted feet around and put them up on her desk. "But ain't he a hunk? I mean like real, genuine, all-world hunk." Her eyes danced a naughty little jig. "My heart could get arrested for speeding anytime he's near."

Even though Jessie had the urge to agree, she fought it. "Well, I hope not to be close to him ever again, in the near or far future." She sat down and pulled over a convenient pile of papers. Anything to get her mind off Ben Adamanti. "Actually never in this life would be soon enough for me."

"That's going to be tough," Marla said. "Or are you skipping the love-in tonight?"

Jessie's entire life, or at least the unpleasant parts, passed before her eyes. Marla was not referring to a sixties-type gathering celebrating love, but rather, to an interdepartmental gathering. Once every quarter, two departments and selected city executives would have dinner on neutral ground for some informal conversation. Now, Jessie knew she was just as understanding of the other guy's point of view as anyone, maybe better. However, there were some people whose attitudes dated back to Genghis Khan.

Was it really his attitude or the way he made her heart race? a little voice asked. What absolute nonsense, she answered back to that silly muse. Any racing of the heart or weakening of the knees was due to the stale doughnut she'd had for breakfast.

"The love-in can't really be with the juvenile division," Jessie argued, though she knew the answer. In fact, there on her desk, right on top of the biggest stack of forms, sat the letter inviting her to the event. "Improve your relations with the juvenile division, reach a closer understanding of their problems," the paper read. Great, just great. With her luck—

"I've already talked to Ethel about sitting next to Mr. Super Fantastic," Marla told her. "It's costing me three weekends of being on call, but it'll be worth it to stare into those deep brown eyes of his all evening."

"Blue," Jessie said.

Marla frowned.

"His eyes are blue," Jessie explained. Then, seeing Marla's eyes narrow, she was sorry she had. "It's hard not to notice when he spends a whole morning glaring at you."

"And you pretend your heart doesn't go pitter-patter when you're near Mr. Macho Cool," Marla said with a smirk as she went back to her work. "I knew that beneath that cool exterior beats the heart of your average red-blooded young woman."

Jessie considered arguing that statement, but decided it wasn't worth it. Especially since there was a more important issue to take care of—getting Ethel to arrange for Jessie to sit next to someone safe.

"Why didn't you change?" Marla asked when they stepped into the lobby of the Tippecanoe Place. "I wouldn't have minded waiting."

"I didn't think there was time," Jessie said with a shrug. She'd dropped her car off at home and had had Marla pick her up. "Besides, Tommy O'Rourke doesn't mind if I come casual."

"You're partnering with him?" Marla shook her shoulder-length blond hair. "He's a sweetheart, as grandfathers go. But certainly not someone to bring some sparkle and excitement to a young girl's dreams."

Jessie ignored her co-worker's words as the hostess led them through the foyer and up the huge staircase leading to the second floor. The opulent mansion had been the home of the founder of an automobile company, but was now the finest restaurant in South Bend, Indiana. Either way, to Jessie it still felt like the setting for some fairy tale—knights rushing in to save fair maidens, kisses releasing spells that held handsome princes prisoner. Silly tales that had no relationship to reality.

"I don't know why we have to hold the meeting here," Jessie grumbled. "The Dew Drop Inn would do just as well, and that's where most of us eat anyway."

"Would you lighten up?" Maria scolded her. "This is a great place."

Jessie just glared at the red velvet drapes hanging at the ten-foot windows as they were led into a private parlor where the rest of the juvenile officers and social workers were already seated.

"You have to sit where your place cards are," Ethel said.

Jessie suppressed a frown. Was that a smirk on her supervisor's face? No, it couldn't be. Not sweet, grandmotherly Ethel. Yet there were only two empty chairs left. One was in the middle by a tall, lean, blond man whom she didn't recognize, and the other was at the end of the table by—

"Marla, you sit here by Mr. Diemers," Ethel said, indicating the chair by the blonde. "Ron's new to the area and I thought you could give him tips about apartments."

If Marla was sitting there, then that only left the empty seat next to Ben Adamanti. The murmur of voices faded to background noise as Jessie wished she could hide. With her chair at the end as it was, there was no one to her right and just Ben to her left. It was going to be tough to ignore him all evening. Jessie took a deep breath and forced herself to nod to Ben as she walked over to take her place.

"So we meet again," he said.

"Small world," Jessie said through her teeth.

Ben stood up to pull out her chair. "Looks like the pleasure's all mine," he murmured, bending close. Almost but not quite close enough to brush her ear.

His breath felt warm on her neck, like the caress of the summer sun. She swallowed hard to will the image away and sat down. "Thank you," she said.

Ben smiled at her. "Like I said, the pleasure's all mine."

Jessie felt a strange fire creeping over her cheeks, an unwelcome response to the way his eyes seemed to caress her, the way the depth of his voice seemed to glide along her heart. She couldn't stop her blush any more than she could drag her gaze from his.

"Hey, hey," Tommy O'Rourke called down. "What's going on down there?"

"Probably something they don't want us to know about," Ethel snickered.

Jessie found the strength to pull her eyes from Ben's and let them sweep the sea of grinning faces around the table. She'd finished her growing up here in South Bend, the last two years of high school and college. Most of the time she liked meeting friends no matter where she went, but once in a while—and this was one of them—she wouldn't mind being a faceless cipher in a big city.

"I don't care how it looks now, if anyone needs a love-in, it's those two," someone said.

"Yeah, you should have heard them this morning. With all their yelling, they woke up the guys at the main fire station."

"I think they should kiss and make up."

"Absolutely. That would set the proper tone for this meeting."

Jessie tried to ignore them all, attempting to radiate dignity and decorum, but it didn't work. Smiling eyes ringed her like wolves cornering their prey. She felt trapped. Her stomach tightened, but it didn't feel much like fear or annoyance.

Ben leaned closer, his soft words tickling her ear. "If we play it tough, they'll keep this up all night. If we kiss, they'll turn their attention to something else."

Jessie felt the watchful gazes still on her and knew that he was right. If she refused to kiss him, it would turn into a battle of wills and make her seem prudish and ill-humored.

"All right," she murmured in reply. "But just one."

"Hey, no problem. I can only take so much punishment myself."

What was that supposed to mean? But before she could fix him with a good glare, he laid his lips gently, ever so gently, on hers. His touch was as soft as starlight, yet with the power of a jolt of lightning. Jessie felt as if she'd landed in a safe harbor and at the same time, as if she'd been dropped in the middle of a bonfire of passion and deep yearnings. Her mind was a whirl of conflicting thoughts, but her heart wanted only to read the promises in those lips. He began to pull away, and she leaned with him, putting a hand on his chest.

Songs danced in her heart, and laughter and sunshine blossomed in the air. The touch of his mouth spoke magic into her soul, awakening dreams and delights from a distant slumber. She felt young and alive with the first blush of spring, coming to life after a long and harsh winter. For the moment there was nothing but wonder and warmth, slow-spreading flames that crept along, surrounding her heart. Then he moved away to breathe in her ear.

"Ah, ah," he murmured. "Just one. You promised."

His mockery was nothing compared to the scolding she was about to give herself. What kind of an idiot was she turning into?

"I just wanted to make sure that you didn't turn it into a six-hour single," she whispered, trying to save face. "I'm starving and I don't want to miss dinner."

Luckily any comments he might have chosen to make were drowned out by the enthusiastic clapping of their coworkers, and then the waitresses were there to take drink orders. Jessie managed to order a blush Chablis while Ben had a cabernet.

Once the waitresses had left, it seemed that everyone at the table had something to say, everyone but Jessie and Ben, that is. She sat in uncomfortable silence that seemed to grow louder by the moment. She did not like this man, she told herself. She was not attracted to him and she had not enjoyed his kiss. The words echoed about in mockery, and she was quite glad to see the waitress arrive with the drinks.

Ben raised his glass to her. "May our people live in peace."

She raised her own glass. "Until the mountains sink into the earth and the rivers run dry."

Then a quick sip of wine and silent congratulations on how well she did.

Tommy O'Rourke and Ethel made some welcoming comments for their respective departments that Jessie only half listened to. Why was Tommy doing the speaking for the juvenile division? He'd been there the longest, but Ben was head. She didn't want to say it was a thoughtful thing of Ben to do, but she couldn't think of any other reason.

Jessie suddenly felt Ben's eyes on her and she turned quickly to better face the speakers. Unfortunately that brought her knee up against Ben's leg. Her first inclination was to pull away, but that was ridiculous. She wasn't a timid maiden who'd never been near a man before. She refused to notice the contact, refused to think how muscled his leg was.

Once the speeches were over, Ethel introduced Ron Diemers as the new manager of the county's data processing service and major addition to the area's bachelor pool, then the larger group dissolved into smaller conversation groups.

Jessie and Ben seemed to be off by themselves, excluded by the others. She sipped at her wine, frantically thinking of some scintillating topic of conversation.

"That's a pretty wine."

Startled, Jessie looked at her glass and then at Ben. What in the world was he talking about?

"The blush," he explained. "It matches the one in your cheeks."

Whatever blush was there, deepened about ten shades and got about a hundred degrees hotter. But she was not going to fall prey to his smooth tongue or to the sudden wild images that he'd conjured up.

She desperately searched for an area she could compliment. Not that he didn't provide her with sufficient material. Bushy, almost curly brown hair. Bright blue eyes, burning with life. Broad shoulders, slim waist. A tough, craggy face that was touched with the most curious of smiles. But she wasn't sure it was safe to get into any of that. She looked at his glass of wine.

"Your wine matches your cheeks, too," she said.

He looked at his glass of rich, robust, red liquid.

Jessie tried but couldn't fully suppress a laugh. "Well, it did this morning when you were mad and hollering at me."

He stared at her, eyes open wide in surprise. "That was cruel."

But it kept her safe. "Just a little," she agreed.

"Little?" he exclaimed. "It was downright vicious. Mean, stomp-a-man-while-he's-down vicious."

"So was the way you were yelling this morning."

"Was it?"

Suddenly the dancing laughter was gone from his eyes, and she could have sworn they shone with worry. He took her hand and that feeling of safety came rushing back to surround her.

"I didn't mean to yell," he said. "I just have strong beliefs that seem to sometimes take control of my mouth."

What would it be like to take control of that mouth? Or to let it take control of her? It was not a thought to be pursued.

"So I noticed," she said, and greeted the arrival of her salad with the same fervor a drowning victim gave a lifeguard. This place, with its fairy-tale atmosphere, was making her crazy.

Somehow the lettuce provided sanity and she could talk about the Cubs and what kind of football team Notre Dame would have in the fall. By the time her main course arrived to provide additional protection, she had discussed sailing on Eagle Lake in the summer and the hiking trails in Potato Creek State Park.

All interesting topics—light yet not intrusive on any personal secrets. She ended the meal with a sigh of relief. She felt as weary as if she'd run a marathon, but also satisfied that she hadn't fallen into the trap of his eyes again.

Fortunately there were no after-dinner speeches, so once everyone was finished eating, there was just a general round of goodbyes. They all walked out to the lobby as a group.

"Uh, Jess," Marla called. "I know I promised you a ride home, but I kind of wanted to show Ron around a little."

Looking for apartments at nine o'clock at night? But Jessie didn't question it. "No problem. I'm sure Ethel can drop me off."

"No problem is right," Ben said. "I will."

Jessie had managed to fight that fluttery feeling in her stomach all evening in the restaurant, but had no faith that it would disappear once they left the opulent surroundings. Certainly not in the tiny enclosures of a car.

"You don't even know where I live," she protested. "It could be the opposite direction from where you're going."

"She lives over in that apartment complex by St. Joseph's Hospital," Marla told him.

"That's not far."

"Nothing is in South Bend," Marla pointed out.

Jessie decided not to make a big deal out of things. It was just a ride home. He was just a fellow city employee. When he offered her his arm as they stepped outside, she slipped hers in. After all, it was a bit dark here on the stairs. No reason to risk tripping.

"You know what I like about a town this size?" he said, looking up at the sky. "You can see the stars."

Jessie looked up at the glorious canopy above them and murmured her agreement. She knew he was from out of town, but she couldn't remember where from. But she wasn't going to ask him. If she asked a question, then he'd asked one in turn. And that question would lead to another and on and on into friendship and intimacy. The forbidden territory. The nighttime silence was much more pleasant.

Ben opened the car door for her and helped her slide in. Before she realized what he was doing, he had her seat belt fastened and was kissing her lightly. A hunger grew in her heart even as her toes curled in her shoes. Then he pulled away, leaving a sweetness hanging in the atmosphere.

"What was that for?" she asked him.

"I knew you'd want to thank me for helping you with the seat belt."

Right, fella. But the lilacs were heavy on the June air and crickets were playing a night chorus over in the bushes. It was too nice a night to be annoyed. Especially since she suspected she was mostly annoyed with herself. She opened her window and inhaled deeply the crisp clean scent of the soft night air.

He was right—she would have wanted to thank him. Just maybe not that way. But one little kiss was hardly a threat to her peace of existence. She thought of the one in the restaurant, of its mind-boggling, heart-pounding effects. All right, two little kisses. She laid her head back and closed her eyes, letting the silence of the night surround her. She wasn't falling apart, no need to worry.

After a few minutes she opened her eyes to watch Ben drive. He handled the car with a strong confidence that seemed a part of him. The main boulevards were quiet, but his policeman's eye roved about constantly, checking the street corners and darkened doorways. She felt ultimately safe with him, a strange realization and not necessarily a welcome one. Safety was something you achieved by being strong yourself, not from relying on others. She was relieved to see that they were pulling up in front of her apartment. Just as well, she scolded herself lightly. Her reactions had been off base all evening. Time to put herself back together in the proper order.

He stopped the car and went around to open her door. Time to put an end to this little fairy-tale evening.

"I know the way," she said.

"I give door-to-door service."

He helped her out of the car, putting an arm around her waist as if it belonged there. He didn't hug or squeeze, yet somehow she knew his strength, and giving in to an unfamiliar yearning, she leaned heavily into him. It seemed so comfortable and natural, she argued with her subconscious. Why fight it for the last few moments? She could turn her sanity back on with her living-room lights.

Ben took her key silently from her hand, opened the door and quickly glanced around inside. Another little chunk of her heart sighed and relaxed in the exquisite luxury of being protected. Ben returned her keys with another kiss.

This time his touch was rougher, hungrier. Her soul leapt in response to his lips, opened to the pressure of his tongue.

Stars danced in the sky above them, and the gentle summer breeze sang a melody of passion as she moved closer into his embrace. The lessons of the past were lost in the shadows of the night. All that mattered was the strength in his arms that held her so tightly and the shattering hungers he awakened in her.

He withdrew his lips from hers, then slowly put her away from him. It gave her fragile heart time to regroup, to gather in the tattered remnants that had broken free of their bonds. A deep breath steadied her.

"Now what am I thanking you for?" she asked.

Ben shook his head slightly. "I was thanking you."

"How do I tell the difference?"

He kissed her again, but a lot quicker than before, as if he couldn't fight the temptation of her lips. The fires that had been smoldering deep in her soul burst into flame that threatened to engulf her.

"Practice," he said, whispering into the night air. He gently pushed her inside, closing the door after her.

Jessie bolted her door and breathed a sigh of relief as she gazed about her small living room. Sanity would come just as soon as her knees stopped wobbling, she assured herself.

Two

"I'll be home around ten tonight," Jessie told Captain Kidd, the one-eyed cat following her into the kitchen. She grabbed a bunch of grapes from the bowl on the counter and picked up her briefcase. "Your sandbox is clean, your water dish full, and there's enough dry food to last you a week."

She was sure that Captain was about to grunt his thanks but she didn't have time to stay around to hear them. She closed and bolted her door, then hurried outside to her car. The sun was warm and the breeze gentle, a perfect morning for a bruised and aching heart.

She shook her head as she unlocked the car door. What a silly thought. She wasn't bruised and aching, not anymore, not for a long time now. Instead of dredging up the past to cast shadows on today, she should be pleased that last night had turned out so pleasantly.

Jessie pulled into the street, humming softly with a song on the radio. Ben was a riot. And what a line he had. That kiss is you thanking me. And this kiss is me thanking you. We'll have to practice a lot so you can tell the difference.

She smiled to herself. She bet that he was just full of lines. A man for all lines. Just the type of man she liked best—no temptation to take any of it seriously.

She turned onto Main Street as the tune on the radio ended. "Lots of news coming up," the deejay informed the world. "Right now it's 7:45 in the a.m. Temp's seventy-two degrees and should get up to eighty-eight. But let's take a peek back and see what happened on June 3 in history."

Jessie's breath caught in her throat, and she snapped the radio off, but it was a futile gesture. The date hung in the air like a storm waiting to break. And it wasn't as if she hadn't known it was coming. Better to face it now and face it down, she told herself. She had a lot more June 3s to get through in her life, and she could handle them.

She stopped for a red light and closed her eyes briefly. Fourteen years ago today, a child had been born, a little girl who Jessie liked to imagine had her brown eyes and curly hair, and every year since, Jessie had given that child a present. On that very first birthday, Jessie had given her daughter parents who could take care of her and love her. Since then, she'd given her lots of other things—a tricycle, a puppy and enough love to fill the universe. They'd all been given from deep within Jessie's heart and imagination. This year she'd give her daughter a telephone of her very own. Maybe a cordless one that made it easier to flop across your bed while whispering confidences to your very best friend in all the world. She could almost hear the girl's squeal of delight when she opened the gift and her pleading that they plug it in right away so she could make a call.

Jessie smiled. She hoped her daughter had lots of friends and that those confidences were over nothing more serious than yesterday's history test or a new dress she wished for.

A child born of such pain should know nothing but sunshine in her life.

Jessie pulled into the parking lot as a shadow crossed her heart. She hoped, too, that her daughter hadn't inherited Jessie's weakness for blue-eyed men. Of course, it wasn't just Randy Parnell's blue eyes that had been her downfall when she had been barely sixteen. Her mother's recent death to cancer had rocked Jessie to the core, and she had needed someone to love, a knight in shining armor who would ride through White Pigeon, Michigan, and rescue her from her grief.

Unfortunately, besides devastating blue eyes, Randy also had the morals of a jackrabbit. By the time Jessie realized that he was taking advantage of her grief and threw him out of her life, she was pregnant. Marrying him was out of the question, but so was keeping the child, her father made her see. They didn't have anything left after her mother's death—not energy, not happiness, not money. So she gave birth, then she gave the child away.

She saw her daughter once, that tiny bit of life that had grown beneath her heart for nine months. Her baby's skin was red, her eyes were shut tight, and she was crying her lungs out. Jessie cried, too, with love that was bursting inside her for this tiny being, and with rage at Randy and his promises of love and caring. Love had done this to her—brought her to this point of giving up her heart and her soul—her love for Randy that made her believe in him, and his physical loving that gave her this tiny baby in the first place. Love was what had broken her spirit.

Jessie blinked back the wetness in her eyes as she parked her car and briskly walked across the lot, shoulders back and head high. Things were fine now. Dad had remarried and was retired in Plymouth. Her younger sister, Denise, was living in Elkhart with her husband and their three children, while her older brother, Danny, was teaching at a junior college in Texas.

And her child—she was living with a good family of her own somewhere in the Midwest. It wasn't just the only thing to do; it was the right thing. Jessie knew it and that's why she never let herself think about that time, except on June 3, when the memories were too strong to fight.

Jessie pushed open the door to her office. "Good morning, good morning, good morning, all." She moved quickly to her desk. It was going to be a full day with lots of other kids needing her help. Time to put the past behind her for another year.

"Good morning," Ethel said. "I see you made it home all right."

"Why wouldn't I have?" Jessie asked. "Ben's a policeman. He knows the city quite well."

Ethel just smiled and turned back to her paper. "I see."

Jessie tried not to give in to the frown that threatened to capture her lips and put her purse in the side drawer of her desk. As she turned, she caught Marla smiling at her.

"You look rather chipper this morning," the other woman said, arching an eyebrow.

"A person is normally chipper after they've had a good night's sleep."

"Or a good night not sleeping," Marla suggested.

Jessie had no reason to blush, but felt a fire covering her cheeks. "I was in my apartment ten minutes after we left the restaurant," she said. "Alone."

"Too bad," Marla said.

Jessie's phone rang and she grabbed it up. She didn't need a long discussion on priorities with Marla this morning. "Jessie Taylor here."

"Ben Adamanti."

His voice was brisk and businesslike, but still put a little dance on her lips. She dived eagerly into whatever problem he was presenting her with. "What can I do for you?" she asked.

"I was just checking back with you about Robbie Morgan. He's scheduled for his evaluations tomorrow afternoon."

"Good," Jessie said. She pulled her appointment notebook closer and made a notation along the margin. "Will they send me a copy of the results?"

"I listed you on the form," Ben said.

"That should do it, then, though if I don't hear in a day or two, I'll give them a call." The silence hung heavily for a moment, opening the door for Ms. Melancholy to come in. Jessie shut it quickly. "I really appreciate your flexibility in this case. Not everybody would have been willing to change their mind like you did. And I'm really convinced that it's best for Robbie."

"I'm not arguing," Ben pointed out. "Actually I had another reason for calling and was hoping to get a word in edgewise."

Jessie fought the blush that warmed her cheeks, but kept her voice cool. "Oh? How else can I help you?"

A quiet chuckle slid along the phone lines, telling her he could see the blush even if it rested only in her worries. "I was just thinking ahead to lunchtime," he said. "And I was feeling real sad that I might have to eat alone."

Jessie sat on the edge of her desk as indecision seized her soul for a blinding second. She saw before her Ben's laughing blue eyes and forced herself to take a deep breath.

"What a shame," she said quietly. Her voice mirrored her control. She didn't need to date if she didn't want to. And definitely didn't want to, especially not today. "But you're a big boy now and you'll just have to learn how to take care of yourself."

"You don't want to have lunch with me?"

"It isn't that I don't want to." She didn't want him to think it was personal. It wasn't, not really. "But I always have my lunch at the West Side Youth Center."

"Always?"

"Well, if I don't have a meeting," she replied. "And I've already promised them I'd be there. A bunch of us girls are going to have ourselves a hot basketball game."

"You mean slam-dunk, in your face?"

"You got it, fella."

"Maybe some other time," he said.

"Yeah, maybe," Jessie replied. "But my calendar tends to be full."

She hung up slowly and stared at the far wall a long moment. Her calendar was full; that was no lie. And that was the safest way for it to be.

"Over here, Jess," the girl called, waving her hands for the ball. "I'm open."

Jessie threw the ball, then darted the other way to be open for a return pass. She was hot, hungry and getting close to a comfortable exhaustion, just what she liked. The ball came her way again and she leapt to catch it, but it sailed over her head, bounced off the wall and rolled toward the chain-link fence. A young teenage girl with sunglasses stood leaning against the fence near where the ball had come to a stop.

"You want to throw the ball back this way, please?" Jessie called out.

The girl didn't respond at all and, with the dark glasses, it was hard to tell if she'd even heard. Jessie walked over and picked up the ball herself.

"Would you like to join us?" she asked.

This time there was a response. All negative. The girl pushed herself off the fence and stalked into the building. Jessie stared after her a moment and then walked over to the group waiting for her.

"I haven't seen her around here before," Jessie said. "Who is she?"

But the girls all shrugged.

"Don't know."

"She don't talk to nobody."

"She just be around a day or two."

"Mean as a junkyard dog."

"Guess she needs a helping hand," Jessie pointed out as she passed the ball back into the game. The girls were suddenly intent on their game, remembering maybe some of the times they'd needed a helping hand.

But the reminder was all she'd wanted to give them, not an opportunity to brood. "Hey, let's go," she said. A space opened up before her, and she took a shot. The ball missed everything, including the backboard. Nuts, she hadn't been concentrating.

"Air-ball," called a mocking voice.

Everybody stopped and turned, but Jessie knew who it was without looking. Ben. Her heart did some flip-flops before she ordered it to behave.

"Let's see you do any better, Mr. Policeman," one of the girls called out.

"Yeah, fella," Jessie joined in. "Get in the game if you dare."

"I don't have the right kind of shoes," he said, pointing to his leather-soled loafers.

"Chicken," the girls all hooted.

"All right," he said, taking off his sports coat and throwing it across the handrail near the steps. "If that's the way you characters want it."

"Ooh-wee," the girls shouted, pretending to shake.

"I'm not sure you should," Jessie said. But was she concerned that he might slip in those shoes or that her defenses weren't strong enough to withstand his nearness?

"I can take care of myself," Ben said. "You just watch out for yourself."

That's what she was planning on doing. "Oh," Jessie mocked. "Macho man."

"Macho man." The girls doubled up laughing, hugging each other and slapping high-fives.

Ben came over closer, his eyes trying to tease her heart into trusting him. "Now look what you did," he said. "You gave me a nickname. One that I'm not too excited about."

The smile on his lips called her closer, promised her that warmth and safety lay in his arms. She went to retrieve the ball from where it had landed after her errant throw. Distance was what she needed from him. Though that distance made her feel so alone.

"Are we playin' ball or makin' eyes at each other?" one of the girls asked.

"Playin' ball," Jessie said quickly, getting ready to throw the ball in.

"Wait a minute," Ben cried. "Who's on my team?"

They quickly divvied themselves up and got into the action. The ball got passed to Jessie and she took it forward, only to run into a solid wall of Ben. How had he gotten there so quickly?

She tried to pass the ball, but his hands were everywhere. The scent of his after-shave surrounded her, but even as it tried to slow her movements into languor, her heart raced even faster. One of her teammates ran behind her, so Jessie spun, tossing the ball to the girl. But Ben was still there, his body brushing up against hers. Her heart's thudding became a distraction.

"I don't have the ball anymore," she pointed out to him.

"Got to guard against a pass back," he said, though his eyes were on her, not the ball.

Then his team stole the ball, it was passed to him, and Jessie found herself trying to stop him.

"Come on, Jess. Don't let him shoot."

"Get closer to him, girl. He don't bite."

His grin dared her, challenged her to brush against his body as he had against hers. She just guarded him, moving from side to side as he dribbled the ball and waited for his chance to get by. Come in closer, his smile said, trying to lure her once more into his spell. But then her eyes got caught in his, lost in the blue depths that promised delights and wonder, and her feet slowed.

"Wake up, Jess."

She moved just in time to block his play, though he charged into her, nearly knocking her off her feet. His smile vanished and he dropped the ball, grabbing at her so that she didn't fall. His arms were solid and steady. His eyes were close enough to drown in.

"You okay?" he asked.

"Foul."

"You charged into her, man."

"Yeah, I'm fine." Why were her knees about to give way, then? She moved out of his arms, though it felt like leaving the summer sun for the icy chill of winter. "I can take a little charge."

"Little?" one of the girls snorted.

Jessie's team took the ball, and the game went on. Luckily though, it was almost one o'clock. She had only a few more torturous minutes of guarding Ben. Of watching those eyes that seemed able to will warmth and wonder into her very soul. Of seeing those lips that had brought such delight into her evening. She glanced at her watch. Two minutes to, close enough.

"That's it, girls," she called out, and ignored their groaning. "I have to get back to work, and you guys are supposed to do some reading." There were even more groans.

"March," Jessie ordered. "Or I'll tell Mrs. Willis no lemonade and everyone spends the afternoon cleaning out the storeroom."

This time the grumbling protests were muted, and the girls trudged off inside the old schoolhouse that now housed the youth center.

"Boy," Ben said, picking up his jacket. "Were you ever a sergeant in the Marine Corps?"

"Funny," she replied. "Very funny."

The playground seemed small and crowded all of a sudden. His presence was more demanding, more intimidating now when the girls weren't around to provide her safety. She started to walk toward her car.

"Want to go grab a bite to eat?" he asked.

She shook her head, thankful for her established routine. "I'll have a sandwich at my desk," she said. "I need to get my stuff out of the car, take a shower and head back to the office."

He slung his coat over his shoulder and draped his other arm around her shoulders. Part of her reveled at his touch, but her mind knew better. Still, to shrug his arm off would seem prudish, unfriendly. Just because her body wanted to burst into flame at his slightest touch, it didn't mean that he meant to have that effect on her.

"Thanks for my new name," he said. "I really appreciate it."

"It seems to fit quite well."

Blue eyes turned to glare at her. "Is that an insult?"

Actually it wasn't. He was macho, but in all the positive ways—he was a strong, reliable, take-charge sort of man. Someone to depend on, her heart pointed out with a smug little smile. But for how long? her mind countered.

"Not necessarily," she said, but chose not to elaborate.

"I still think I owe you," he said.

They were by her car, and she was able to free herself from the spell of enchantment his smile had put her under. "That's okay."

"No," Ben insisted. "I always pay my debts. How about dinner tonight?"

One part of her jumped for joy, while another part put an anchor on her emotions. This man was potent, more dangerous than Randy and all his stupid lines. Her defenses had been in place for years, and no one had broken through until now. She didn't dare spend more time with him.

"I have a meeting at Adams High after work," she said.

"A long one?"

"No," she admitted slowly. "But I'm teaching a class at seven tonight."

"That should give us time for at least a quick dinner," he said. "After all, we both have to eat."

She leaned back against her car. Her mind was scrambling frantically for some excuse, but her unruly thoughts refused to cooperate. Not when he was so close to her, when she could still taste the feel of his lips on hers.

"I don't know," she said feebly.

"Great," he said, taking her vacillation as acceptance. "I'll call you this afternoon with directions to my place."

"Your place?" This wasn't what she expected, not an intimate meal in the privacy of his home. "Why not the Oaken Bucket? That's where I usually eat on Thursdays."

"That's only because you haven't tasted my burgers, grilled to order in my backyard."

He moved in closer, and Jessie found it hard to breathe. Fear and excitement warred along her spine. She didn't want him to touch her, didn't want to feel her heart sing when he was near, but oh, how she needed his lips on hers.

Logic was gone, bounced out the door, but it wasn't quite happiness that took its place. How could a man she barely knew awaken hungers she'd kept buried for years? Not that she cared to discuss the question, not when there were lips to be met and sweetness to be shared.

She moved into his arms and felt the earth shake. His lips demanded that she melt in his arms, and she obeyed. Closer and closer she moved into his embrace, willing his arms to tighten further, willing the fires in her to be answered in him. His touch was magic, everything that life should hold.

Then suddenly her common sense threw her back to earth, and she pulled away. It wasn't a very fast or a very determined effort, but she did manage to break free of his arms.

"Well, tonight then?" he said.

She just nodded, incapable of speaking, incapable of refusing. Then he was gone and so was her chance to tell him she wasn't interested in a relationship, that she was happy as she was.

Three

The coals looked just about right, so Ben put the hamburgers onto the grill. "How do you like your burgers?" he called over to Jessie.

She was sitting in the sun on his chaise longue, the back cracked about halfway down. Her eyes closed and face relaxed, she looked totally at peace.

"Medium," she answered, not bothering to move even an eyelid.

"Medium rare, medium exactly or medium well?"

Her eyes opened slightly at that, slits barely concealing the laughter that lurked behind them. "Just try for a medium medium."

A soft smile curled her lips as her eyes went back to closed.

"You doubt me?"

The smile bubbled up into a soft chuckle. "I'm just overwhelmed."

Ben seasoned the patties on the grill, feeling his own smile grow. He loved having people over, company to laugh with, though Jessie wasn't just anybody. He sensed that she was a kindred spirit, someone he could have a real friendship with. The past had taught him a lot of lessons, the most important of which was to enjoy the little things like an evening of laughing and joking with Jessie. But was an evening spent in the company of such a beautiful lady a little thing? He put the char-broiled meat on waiting buns, picking up the plates before turning toward Jessie.

"Come on, sleepyhead. Time to eat."

"I'm not sleeping," she said, sitting up. "I was just resting my eyes."

Ben just smiled. "You've got coleslaw, baked beans and some tortilla chips. Plus there's an assortment of guck to cover your burger with."

"What kind of food is tortilla chips?"

"They're made out of cornmeal."

"I know what they're made of," Jessie said. "It's just that I didn't know this was going to be a junk-food potluck."

"The tortillas are unsalted," he protested. "That way they're not really junk food."

Skepticism flooded Jessie's face. "Interesting," she replied. "With your ability to cut such fine points you should have been a lawyer."

"That's a terrible thing to say," Ben said. "And here I thought we were friends."

"Sorry," she murmured softly. "I didn't know you were such a tender heart."

"I am," he replied. "I really am."

"I'll try to remember that the next time you bellow at me."

"I don't bellow," he protested. "I just get my point across."

Jessie grinned and he had to laugh with her. She was one tough cookie, could take it as well as dish it out. He felt comfortable with her. There were none of the usual first-date tension and awkward silences. Did that mean that they were so well suited or that this wasn't really a first date? Not that it mattered to him. All he was looking for was some pleasant company.

"Another glass of wine?" he asked.

Jessie shook her head. "If you remember, I have a meeting and then I have to teach a class. I can't afford to fall asleep in my own lecture. If I should happen to snore, I'd lose the little bit of respect I'm afforded now."

He finished his own glass of wine. "Know what I like about you?" he asked. "You can laugh at yourself."

Her frown was only half-serious. "You mean it's not my great looks or my brilliant intellect? What a blow!"

He looked across the table, his gaze sliding over her. Hair that longed to be mussed, a mouth that was full and ready for the kissing and a body that could light sparks in him without half trying. "Well, now that you mention it, there a few other parts that are worth noticing."

Something in his voice must have reflected the sudden flame in his soul, for she looked uncomfortable. Her soft brown eyes grew shadowed as she got to her feet. "We'd better get this stuff put away. I'm going to have to be going soon."

"You don't have to help," Ben protested. "Sit and relax while you can."

But it was as if she hadn't heard him. She piled the condiments on a tray and carried them into the kitchen. She grabbed the bag of tortilla chips and the bowl of coleslaw.

She seemed more at ease inside, putting away the catsup and mustard as if the refrigerator were some sort of shield.

"I'm surprised that you own a house," she said.

He took a container out of a cabinet, glancing over at her in surprise.

"I mean bachelors-about-town aren't usually into home maintenance, yard work and that kind of thing."

He spooned the coleslaw into the container. "I was married before," he replied. "I guess I got used to the freedom of having my own place."

"Not all divorced men would consider home ownership freedom. You can't spend your weekends partying if you have to mow the lawn."

He pretended surprise. "You've never been to a lawn-mowing party?"

Her laughter was like new-fallen snow—crisp, sparkling and refreshing. There was also something about it that made him wonder if it was rare. She didn't seem to be a woman who laughed very much; not deep, honest laughter fresh from the soul.

"I guess the extra space and a yard of your own would be nice," she said. "But I'm not sure that I'd be willing to pay the price of keeping it up."

Her soft voice seemed to pry open a door that suddenly cast light where there had been darkness, a door he wasn't sure he wanted open. He put a clip on the bag of tortilla chips and went back outside for the rest of the stuff. She followed him out to collect their plates and, though there was nothing about her that said she was waiting, he felt himself give in.

"I enjoy having a place of my own," he said as if it explained everything, yet knowing it didn't. "I never even had a room of my own until I got out of the army."

There were no words of sympathy forthcoming, for which Ben was grateful, but Jessie didn't really need to say anything. The sincerity of her caring spirit hung over the yard like the humid beginnings of a summer storm. Ben cleared his throat, making a loud and rough sound.

"Things weren't that stable in my youth," he said. "I bounced around a bit. Different friends and relatives." Ben shrugged his shoulders. "Most of the places I landed barely had enough room for the people already there."

He picked up their glasses and silverware, almost afraid to look at Jessie. A bleeding heart like her would have sympathy overflowing her eyelids like the St. Joseph River overflowed its banks after a wet spring, and he didn't want it. He pushed open the back door and dumped everything on the counter.

"Want to do the dishes now?" she asked. Her voice wasn't as lilting as usual, but neither was it dripping with pity, for which he was grateful.

"Nah, I can do them later. Let's take a walk down by the river. Wake you up a little so that you don't fall asleep in your lecture."

"Sounds great."

He took a key, a bag of bread crusts and her hand, and left his shadowed melancholy back in the kitchen with the dirty dishes. They walked along the tree-shaded sidewalk for several minutes of healing silence. Jessie seemed interested in the old homes lining the narrow brick streets, while he breathed deeply of the lilacs that permeated the June air around them.

"I love these old sections of town," she said.

"Yeah."

"I don't know how anybody can live in the suburbs," she said. "They're so inconvenient and totally without character."

"Yeah," he agreed.

He could feel her looking closely at him. "You certainly have a silver tongue."

He stuck it out at her before defending himself. "Hey, you were doing a good job carrying the conversation. I didn't want to butt in."

"Not only are you a tender soul, but you are a gentle one, as well."

"That's right."

They turned at Lafayette Street and walked north toward the river. "I certainly wouldn't want to stay there," Ben said as they passed the hospital.

"Why not?" Jessie asked. "I hear it's a very good hospital."

"Yeah, but there are too many quacks around," he said, indicating the duck pond just across an open space of parkland.

Jessie groaned loudly. "And here I thought your silence meant you were brooding over the sorrows of divorced life."

Right reading of his mood, just wrong reason. "It wasn't as hard as some," he said. "We didn't have any kids or long, drawn-out battles. We had just grown apart."

"It still can be painful."

He stopped at the fence of the duck pond and leaned on it, watching the ducks race over to greet them. "I guess," he said. "Though most learning experiences are painful to some extent. Seems that man needs a little pain in order to impress upon him the seriousness of the issue."

"Sounds like going to the principal's office," she said with a laugh. "Or an after-school detention."

He reached into his bag of bread crusts and gave her a handful before scattering some of his own. The ducks raced about, grabbing up pieces of bread. "Actually that's what it felt like," he admitted, and made his voice deeper and gruffer. "'Little Ben Adamanti, haven't you learned your lesson yet? Love is not something you can depend on for the long haul or for the hard times.'"

Jessie laughed and took some more crusts from the bag. "Certainly not for the hard times," she agreed.

There was no shock or concern in her voice, nothing but real, honest agreement. He felt himself relax as he hadn't for ages. "It's not that I'm against love," he said. "It's good for Valentine's Day and the movies."

"It's like candy," she said. "A little bit brings some sweetness into your life, but too much gives you cavities."

Ben found that his smile reached from somewhere deep within. He couldn't believe his good fortune. He'd found a lovely lady who understood his philosophy on love, a lovely, charming lady with a happy, positive outlook on life.

He watched her as she tossed bread to the ducks, making sure that the pieces landed at different places so that they all had a chance to get some. Lovely, charming and with a strong sense of justice.

"She could never understand my devotion to my job," Ben said suddenly. "My long hours were making a difference, but she wanted me home at regular times, thought I could run on a nine-to-five schedule if I wanted."

Jessie nodded. "Some jobs can be left at the office, but others can't. You sleep and wake up with them. They take everything from you, so that there's nothing left to share at times. That's when you need support, not more demands."

"Something tells me you've been through a divorce, too," Ben said, giving her the last of the bread.

The look she gave him was one of surprise. "Nope, didn't need to be burned to learn not to play with fire."

He wasn't sure how to read that remark, but his fingers reached over to run lightly over hers. He could feel the tingle that ran through her. It was like an electric charge with enough energy and power to light up a good section of downtown South Bend. Could she feel it, too? Did she want to acknowledge its existence?

Even as he had the thought, Jessie turned toward him. She wasn't actually moving into his arms, but once they opened, she was there. Her softness pressed against him, her heart pounding away in rhythm with his. He bent down, his lips taking hers hungrily.

She was soft and moist, strength and power, yet fire enough to send him up in flames. He felt all-powerful, holding her in his arms. There was nothing he couldn't do, no battle he couldn't win, yet all he wanted was to hold her tighter and let her warmth weave a tighter spell around his innermost being.

They parted for lack of air, but also because something deeper was happening. He could sense the stillness in the evening, but not the reasons, just that they were very good together.

"I'd better be going," she said. "The dinner was great. Thanks."

"We'll have to do it again sometime soon," he said. His hands took one of hers prisoner, conveying another language with his touch.

"Soon," she agreed.

"All right, now tell all," Denise insisted. "I know something exciting's going on in your life."

Jessie frowned at her sister as they maneuvered around the mall directory sign. "What are you talking about?"

"You've got an extra sparkle to your eyes, a lilt to your voice and a healthy glow in your cheeks. Plus you bought a gorgeously slinky dress, the likes of which I've never seen on you."

"Jeez," Jessie exclaimed. "It was on sale and too good to pass up. As for the so-called glow—I'm young and healthy, it hasn't rained for almost a week and summer's here. What am I supposed to do? Walk around all slumped over with a winter pallor to my cheeks?"

"You're not going to tell me about him."

"There's nothing to tell." Jessie made no attempt to control the exasperation in her voice. "Hey, they've got some bathing suits in there."

Denise was distracted as Jessie had hoped, and hurried into the store to check out the bathing suits. Going shopping with her sister was fun, but her inquisition was getting a wee bit tiresome. Every time Jessie did something a little differently, Denise was certain there was a man in her life. As if Jessie's life couldn't be happy and complete with just her work to keep her occupied. Denise was sometimes so old-fashioned, Jessie found it hard to believe her sister was three years younger than her.

"I don't think so," Denise said as she came back over to join Jessie. "I just don't have the figure for cutaway suits. Not after three kids. Much as I love them, having them does tend to ruin your figure, not to—"

Denise stopped, her face a picture of guilt and anguish. "Oh, I'm sorry, Jess. I didn't mean to remind you."

Jessie just made a face as she stopped to check out an overpriced T-shirt. "For goodness' sake, you don't have to apologize for an innocent remark. And I'm sure that having three kids is much harder on your figure than one."

"Actually it's probably more the fact that I finish all their food," Denise admitted. "Speaking of which, what do you say we go get some ice cream?"

"Denise," Jessie cried, her voice mixing laughter in with exasperation. But whatever else she was going to say was lost as she looked up and saw Ben coming toward them.

"I thought that was you," he said. "Finding many bargains?"

"A few," she said slowly, cautiously. His blue eyes seemed to pull her into their depths, will her to drown in their cool intensity.

"I'm Denise Spencer," Denise said. "Jessie's sister."

Her sister's voice knocked Jessie back into the world. "I'm sorry, sis. This is Ben Adamanti. Captain Ben Adamanti. He's head of the juvenile division."

"And hamburger chef extraordinaire." He held out his hand to Denise. "Pleased to meet you, Denise."

Denise's eyes had a definite sparkle to them as she shook Ben's hand. Her quick glance at Jessie promised a complete interrogation once they were alone.

"So you and my sister work together?" Denise asked.

"Among other things."

Jessie wanted to groan aloud, but decided that would be playing right into his hands. And wouldn't that be fun? a little voice asked.

"To be honest," Jessie said. "We've clashed over a few cases and played on opposing basketball teams over at the youth center."

"And I tried to help Jessie when she locked her keys in her car," Ben added.

"Are you still doing that?"

Denise's voice was scolding, and Jessie couldn't help but send a frosty glance over Ben's way. He had to tell that, didn't he? The gaze he telegraphed to her was steady with a hint of a challenge. She wasn't sure she wanted to know what he was challenging her to do, but was certain she wasn't going to take him up on it.

"Old habits die hard," Jessie said as much to Denise as to herself. "So what are you doing here at the mall? Looking for early summer bargains?"

"Actually I came for the show," he said, nodding toward the large open area at the center of the mall. "It's amateur night tonight, and some of the acts are pretty good. You ladies staying for it?"

Jessie shook her head. "Afraid not. Denise's baby-sitter has to get home early. She can't stay much longer."

Denise gave Jessie a real frown, but she didn't come right out and dispute her words. "But you could stay," Denise said to Jessie ever so sweetly. "There's no need for both of us to rush away."

Ben looked expectantly over at Jessie, and she felt like she'd been tossed up on stage. "No, I really have to get home," she said. "This is my first early evening this week, and there's so much I need to do."

She let her voice trail off, as if she could list all the chores awaiting her if somebody wanted her to, but no one seemed to. Though Denise's frown had increased in intensity, Ben seemed to take her refusal without pain.

"You're going to miss Steve Quinn, South Bend's fireman-comic," he told her. "When he's rich and famous, you're going to be sorry."

"If I don't do some laundry, I'm going to be sorry tomorrow," she said, though staying another hour would hardly put her in the desperate range when it came to clothes for tomorrow.

Why not stay, then? she asked herself. Ben was good company; she'd seen that for herself the couple of times they were together. Perhaps too good. It wouldn't hurt for her to start using her brain and not her heart here.

"Well, I'd better get going if I want to find a seat," he said, and nodded to Denise. "Nice meeting you."

"I hope to see you again," Denise said. Her look toward Jessie was pointedly obvious.

"See you soon," Jessie said to Ben.

"I'm taking that as a promise," he said.

She just smiled and, taking Denise's arm, pulled her in the other direction. She knew it was too much to hope that her sister would not challenge her decision, but at least they could be out of Ben's hearing before she did so.

"What's this nonsense about my baby-sitter?" Denise demanded. "Larry's with the kids. You know, my husband and their father. And he doesn't have to go anyplace tonight."

"I just thought you'd be anxious to get back home to your family," Jessie replied, turning on her heel and walking toward the parking lot.

Denise followed along not saying anything until they were outside. "He looks like a nice guy."

Jessie shrugged. "Sometimes."

"Sometimes?"

"We've had some disagreements." Then quickly continued, in answer to Denise's questioning eyes. "We don't always agree on how to best handle some of the problem kids."

"No big deal," Denise said. "I'm sure cops and social workers naturally disagree at times. They look at things from a different perspective."

Jessie tried to remember which row their cars were parked in. Oh, right, the one two rows over.

"You got to learn to lighten up, little sister."

It would be easy to be light in those arms. With the size of Ben's biceps, Jessie was sure that he could lift her without blinking an eye.

"I date and go out," Jessie said.

"Oh, yeah?"

"I do," Jessie snapped. "It's not like I do something every night, but then most people with demanding careers don't."

The walk to the cars was silent and strained. Denise put her bags in her trunk, then stopped to stare at her sister.

"It's nice of you to be concerned about all those kids, Jessie. But you can't change the world, and your baby has been someone else's responsibility for a long time now."

Oh, Lord, another of these lectures. "I don't even think about her," Jessie assured her. "She and the girl that gave birth to her are from another time and another world."

"Then why aren't you thinking of a family of your own?"

"How do you know I'm not?"

"Maybe I should have said it was time you started a family of your own."

They stared at each other, both with challenge and determination in their eyes, neither one about to give in. Jessie knew Denise meant well, but what spelled happiness for her sister didn't necessarily spell it for Jessie. A car cruised by, obviously looking for a parking spot, and broke the duel.

"Give Larry and the kids my love," Jessie said.

Denise grunted and walked around to get in the car. "Don't work too hard."

Jessie just smiled, waiting until her sister pulled out of the space and started down the aisle. Then she walked down to her car a few spaces beyond. She tossed her bags in the back seat, but couldn't seem to get into the car herself. It was such a beautiful evening, warm with a touch of sweetness in the air. She had a yearning for laughter, for someone whose hand she could hold while they kept the silence of the night away for a few hours. The idea of her apartment seemed like a desert suddenly; the mall was an oasis.

"I must be turning into a mallie," she said to herself as she trudged back inside.

But her step got lighter and her smile brighter as she hurried through the shoppers. A reasonable crowd filled the center of the mall. The chairs were all taken, and the overflow filled the open area in front of the stores.

Jessie moved to one side, craning her neck for a glimpse of Ben, but she couldn't see him. Why hadn't she accepted the invitation when he'd made it? Was she afraid that Denise would make more of it than she should? And just what difference would it have made if she had?

But she didn't find any answers in her mind or Ben in the crowd. The first act came on, a string quartet from a local junior college. They were quite good, but the lightness of their melodies seemed to make her own heart feel darker, and once the applause died out, she slipped away. She should have known better than to come back.

"I still feel silly," Jessie said. "We could have done without Ben."

"If you like humiliation." Marla readjusted her baseball cap so that it mussed her hair up the least amount, then picked up a softball. "Come on, let's warm up."

Jessie obediently went to stand behind home plate in her catcher's position, and caught the ball Marla threw to her. Their coed softball team had started the season with a full roster and nice numbers in the win column. But a couple of summer colds and vacations later, they were a predominately female team and were being overpowered by everyone else in the league. Until Marla had decided she'd had enough and signed Ron up to their team, then coerced Jessie into drafting Ben for today's game.

"We don't even know if he's any good," Jessie pointed out.

Marla cut her throwing motion short and glared at Jessie. "With those arms? Girl, if you haven't felt their strength yet, I give up on you."

"Strength and softball skill are two different things," Jessie pointed out.

"Don't nitpick. The man's going to save the day against the Bombers, speaking of which..."

Jessie didn't know if it was Ben or the Bombers who had arrived, but she was silently hoping it was the other team. She wasn't sure she was ready to face Ben yet, not since her disappointing night at the mall. What did she want? Did she even know? She didn't want to need someone so much that she would want to die when he let her down. But did that have to be Ben?

"Boy, if this is our team, we're in trouble," Ben said from somewhere close behind her.

She turned to find herself engulfed in his easy laughter, but she didn't join in. "What's that supposed to mean? I'll have you know I'm a pretty good catcher and Marla's a great second baseman."

He didn't look at all contrite. "I think we need more than the three of us," he said.

"Oh." Why did she always manage to make a fool of herself in front of this guy? She pounded the ball into her mitt a few times. "There's more of us, don't worry."

By this time Marla had come over. "Great you could help us out of this fix," she said. "What position do you play?"

With a raucous amount of horn blowing, the rest of the team arrived and hurried out to the field as the Bombers began warming up over in the outfield. Most of her friends already knew Ben, since the team was basically comprised of employees from social services, and he was quickly accepted and appointed their starting pitcher. After a few more minutes of warm-up, the Bombers took the field and Jessie's team filed into the dugout. Ben sat down next to Jessie.

"So are we going to do the slaughtering or be slaughtered?" he whispered, his breath tickling the soft hairs around her ear.

"Depends on how good you are," she said.

His eyes danced briefly with hers. "I'm good at a lot of things," he said lightly. "Maybe one of these days you should take an inventory of all my skills."

There was a power in his voice, a heady teasing that wasn't all light and mischief. Yet Jessie didn't feel like backing away from it. She laughed and felt a glow growing inside her.

"Let's just concentrate on the ones you apply to softball for now."

Marla was up first and struck out, then Ron popped out to center field before Sally struck out, too. The team took the field, muttering threats that the Bombers just laughed at.

"They always cream us," Jessie told Ben as they went into the infield. "If you've ever dreamed of being a hero, this is your chance."

"Sounds promising. Does the hero get a great reward?"

He picked up a ball, and they tossed it back and forth a few times. Jessie was surprised. Ben threw straight and hard, not feeling that he had to soften his pitches so she could catch them. Jessie found herself answering with harder, faster throws herself.

Ben struck the first Bomber out, then let the second get on base with a grounder that slid past Marla. The next batter bunted, but Jessie was able to throw to first base in time, then the ball went to second to retire the side.

Jessie was grinning as Ben came up to her side. "Maybe it's your skills I should take an inventory of," he said.

His arm went around her shoulders in a companionable gesture, and he stopped by the dugout to help her out of her catcher's pads. That little spark that seemed to ignite whenever he was near hadn't fled, but its flickering glow was like a candle's flame lighting the night. They really could be friends, she realized, enjoying each other's company and sometimes more, but friendship could be the base. It was a good thought, a comforting one. She watched as he went up to take his turn at bat.

"Over the fence, Ben," she called out. "Come on. Let's show 'em how tough we are."

"You didn't have to come out with us after the game," Jessie said.

"There are very few things I do because I have to," Ben replied. "And going out after a softball game with you is not a 'have to.' It's a 'want to.'"

Jessie smiled to herself as she leaned back in the seat of Ben's car, eyes closed to the evening sun they were driving into. She had forgotten that special warmth that being desired, even for an evening, could bring.

The breeze diving in through the open rooftop hatch played with her hair. Summer nights were the sweetest. The lingering heat of the day was seductive, drawing her under its spell. She opened her eyes and found her gaze caught by Ben's hand as it lay on the gear shift. He had such strong hands, safe hands. Hands that would know how to ignite the smoldering heat that slept in her heart on nights like this.

She closed her eyes again, wondering at her thoughts, but not ready to change their direction too much.

"You're quite the Saturday's hero today," she said softly.

"You weren't bad yourself."

Turning her head, Jessie opened her eyes to three-quarters mast. His face looked relaxed, but those policeman's eyes roved the streets before him like a tough pair of beat cops assuring the safety of their world. He was a man a woman could lean on and trust.

"Two home runs, a diving catch and a double play," she said. "That beats my double play and three base hits."

"Don't forget your three RBIs. Shows you're a team player."

"I guess."

But his praise warmed her like the sun warms the sand on the beach. She was a team player in a lot of ways. Giving extra for others had always come naturally to her, but most people just took and never noticed. Maybe Ben did because he was so like her in a lot of ways.

"My teammates would be quite happy to make you a permanent member," Jessie said.

"Fine with me," he replied. "If you want me, too."

Did she? And in just what way? "A couple of the guys are getting transferred," she explained. "That's why they weren't there today. Marla asked Ron, but there's still an open spot if you want it."

He turned momentarily to smile at her. "I don't want to push in. But if you want me, I'm willing and available."

Willing and available for what? It seemed a turning point suddenly, as if he were talking about much more than softball. Her pulse was racing, her soul danced at the thought of his embrace, but her mind screeched on warning brakes. She decided to skirt the issue for a moment.

"My team wants you."

They came to a red light, and he turned to look deeply into her eyes. He wasn't fooled by her fabrication. She was seized by his eyes, seized and pulled deep within them.

Ben wasn't a man to be taken lightly. He seemed able to read beneath the easy phrases she had been hiding behind for years. Did she want to give in to his understanding or back off so that she remained safely behind her walls? No one had so challenged her before, and never was she so tempted to give him the victory.

The light turned green, and the moment of decision seemed to pass. Jessie breathed a sigh of relief. "I'll go along with my teammates," she said offhandedly.

His lips curled in a soft smile. "That's nice," he murmured.

There was a long stretch without lights before them, and Ben's hand reached over to possess hers. She relaxed in his strength. This could be fine; it didn't have to be a threat to her way of life, to her peace of mind. He had learned lessons from his divorce, the same ones she had learned from Randy. He wasn't looking for anyone other than a companion, just as she wasn't. He glanced over at her and she smiled at him.

It was too bad that there wasn't a little gnome in the car, Jessie thought. Someone to take pictures, so that Denise could see that Jessie had her life under control, that she had achieved a comfortable balance of work and recreation. Then maybe her little sister would stop worrying about her.

Not all single people wanted to be married; Jessie certainly preferred her single status. Sure, sometimes she wished she had someone special, someone to go out with, someone to share magical times with. Ben could very well turn out to be that someone special for her. He was strong, fun to be with, yet tender and nonjudgmental. He didn't put any pressures on her and, even though it seemed against her nature, she was starting to trust him.

"Here you are, milady," Ben said as he pulled up in front of her apartment house.

"Thank you, my kind sir."

They faced each other. The fire of passion flared in his eyes, pulling her closer until she felt seared by the heat. Her spirit capitulated to his call, and then her body followed. She sank into his arms, welcoming the taste of his lips on hers.

She wasn't a moth, fearing the flame, but a woman with needs and hungers that matched his. Their mouths clung, and their hearts danced a slow minuet of meeting and pulling away. His arms tightened around her and the dance changed; there was not more pulling away, just the heated rush of hungers.

They pulled apart slowly. Ben's eyes told of his passion, but his lips were in a gentle smile. "I think I'd better be going," he said.

"Yes, I've got some things to do. I'll let you know what our practice schedule for this week's going to be."

He nodded and she got out of the car. Somehow she was losing her fear. Was it being burned away by the heat of their passion or was she finally responding to sound reasoning? No time for commitment didn't have to mean no fun. Maybe she really was getting her life together.

"See you soon," Ben called out.

She waved as he drove off. "I hope so," she told herself as she scurried up to her apartment. "I hope so."

Four

"Just remember, kid." Ben had his face close up to the boy, looking him straight in the eye. "There's a lot of things worse than your momma jawing at you."

This was the second time the twelve-year-old had run away, and each time he was getting closer to the players on the street. What was ahead for this kid scared Ben and he was going to do everything in his power to put a little fear in the boy also.

"People don't always agree, Lenny," Jessie broke in, her voice smooth as silk. "Even people that love each other. The important thing is to talk things out. And if you need help with that, I'm always available."

The defiance in the boy's face softened and he nodded. Ben fought against the urge to lighten his expression. Jessie had a really great idea, suggesting they both sit in on this negotiating session between the boy and his mother. Ben's tough-guy attitude raised the hackles on some kids, but with

Jessie around, they could play nice-cop/tough-cop. Scare the kid a little, but still leave him a way out, a way to save face.

"Thank you, Captain," the boy's mother said. "And Miss Jessie. I don't know what we would have done without you."

They all stood up.

"That's our job, Mrs. Smith," Jessie said. "Just call us a little earlier the next time problems arise."

The woman nodded, then she and Jessie exchanged hugs. The boy shook hands with Ben and left the room with his mother. Ben and Jessie watched them walk down the hallway to the exit. They weren't holding hands, but they were walking closely.

"Hope things work out for them," Jessie said.

"Yeah," Ben replied. "It's tough on her. A single working mother with four kids at home."

"I'm sure Lenny wants to help," Jessie said. "She just has to learn to quit taking out her frustrations on him just because he's the eldest."

Ben looked down at her. Jessie's eyes were filled with sympathy, yet it wasn't paralyzing. He had been wrong about her initially, thinking that she was a good Samaritan who couldn't see reality. She was one tough lady. She couldn't lay her generosity and understanding on the line every day as she did, then be bright and cheerful the next day without possessing a little backbone.

"I think this calls for a celebration," he said.

"We just won a little battle," Jessie warned.

"In our business that's the best we can expect." He gathered up his paperwork and shoved it in a folder to be processed and filed tomorrow.

"It's past eight," he said. "Let's go to Stude's. Get in a little partying."

"I thought you said earlier that you were tired."

"I'm tired of sitting on my can, flapping my jaws all day."

She seemed to hesitate, so he grabbed her arm and started to pull her along. "Come on, lazy bones," he said. "My treat."

"How can I refuse such a charming invitation?" she said, laughing but gathering up her papers and purse to follow him out.

The streets were relatively empty, and they were pulling up to the east side nightclub within a matter of minutes.

"What's this place like?" Jessie asked as they exited the car.

He didn't bother to hide his surprise. "You've never been here before?"

"Is that a crime?" Her tinkling laughter fell gently around him, removing the last few traces of tension from the snarled muscles in his shoulders. "Nightclubs haven't played a large part in my free-time agenda."

"Then it's time someone took you in hand," he said, sliding his arm around her waist to pull her close. She was so strong in character, yet she felt so slight and vulnerable in his arms. He let his lips brush her forehead, not daring to risk further contact.

"I really like the lively crowd they get here," he told her. "Being just down the street from the university, a lot of the night-school students drop by after class. The summer session is smaller than the other semesters, but it's still big enough to put some spark in the local joints."

"Looking for some coeds, Captain Adamanti?" she asked, pinching him on the arm.

"Just for atmosphere," he assured her. "Just for atmosphere."

Easy-listening music greeted them as they walked in the door. The crowd was moderate—probably it would fill up a little more after the last class let out—and the deejay was muted. Ben smiled and led Jessie to an empty table in the far corner. He was in the mood for a little hand holding and slow dancing. He fervently hoped that the lady would agree.

"Rosé all right?" Ben asked as a waitress approached them. "The wine of compromise."

"Compromise?" Jessie laughed at him. "I never thought I'd hear you use that word."

There was something about her smile that seemed to pull him closer, surround him in a way so that he was alone with her, no matter where they were.

"Thanks a lot, lady," he teased back. "You make me sound like a knot-head."

"Poor baby." She patted his hand, but with a quick flick of his wrist, he was holding hers.

"Tricky."

But she didn't pull her hand away, even when the wine came. They savored it along with some silence, watching the few couples dancing and listening to the music.

"You come here often?" Jessie asked.

"Not much," he said. "Sometimes to get something to eat after a seminar at the university. It's pretty much a place for couples in the evenings, and I haven't dated much since I came to South Bend. Too busy, I guess."

Her smile seemed almost sad at the edges. "We have that in common, then," she said. "I've been too busy to date much since I moved here, too."

"I thought you'd lived here for a while," he said.

"Almost fourteen years."

A hundred thousand questions swam in his mind, but he ignored them all. "Fourteen busy years," he said.

Her laughter was starlight, energizing him, giving him courage. "Where'd you come from originally?"

"White Pigeon, Michigan. A small town not terribly far from here."

Ben nodded. "Farm country."

"We lived in town, though. It was a great place to grow up." Her eyes took on new shadows, her voice a different, more tentative timbre. "I had the best of all worlds. A lot of space. Fields and woods to roam around in, but being in town afforded me the benefit of having a lot of friends to play with."

"Sounds good." A bitterness that should have died years ago twisted in his stomach. He stared off into the blackness behind the deejay.

"Yeah, I walked to school and biked all over the place," Jessie went on. "In my child's mind, it was a totally safe world."

"It should be like that for all kids."

"I guess, but it was quite a shock to me when that world fell apart," she said. "Mom got sick with cancer. It was a long illness and expensive. It took a lot out of my father, out of all of us."

The shadows remained, but they were obviously caused by pain. He wanted to reach across, to bring sunshine back into her voice, but something held him back.

"I was fifteen when Mom died. It left me—" Jessie took a deep breath and slowly let it out. "It left me a bit vulnerable."

She still looked vulnerable. She looked fragile and in need of protection. He wanted her in his arms.

"Care to dance?" he asked.

She agreed with an eagerness that flattered, though he suspected it was more of a desire to escape the storm clouds that followed her memories than a hunger for his touch.

Still, out on the dance floor with her in his arms, he could feel a magic growing between them. His hold on her was light, but she swayed against him time and time again. Their bodies pulsed to the rhythm of the music, yet it seemed a deeper, more primitive beat to which their hearts pounded.

"It's your turn now," Jessie said suddenly. "Where are you from?"

A tightness in his belly grew into a full-fledged knot, blotting out his growing need for her, and he couldn't speak. He knew from experience that his memories didn't depress him; they consumed him. He couldn't merely open that door a crack. Some demons exploded in the dimmest light.

"That's okay," Jessie said. "Maybe some other time."

Damn. What kind of man was he? She'd given him a thumbnail sketch of her life, which hadn't all been wine and roses. He should be man enough to do the same.

"I started out in Detroit." He could hear the curtness, the just barely buried anger in his voice, but he couldn't do anything about it.

"Your family traveled a lot?" Jessie asked.

He could read her sympathy, her willingness to listen, and that knot in his stomach seemed to coil even tighter. Was this her professional social worker's attitude? But even as that thought came alive, he crushed it and forced a smile to his lips.

"No, not my family. Just me."

The slow song died, replaced by a fast tune, one he couldn't cope with in his present mood, and he looked toward their table. Jessie nodded and they sat back down. He took a man-size gulp of wine, leaned forward on his elbow and put his tongue back in gear.

"My mother never married my father," he told her. "And single parenthood wasn't her cup of tea, so she tossed me out into the relative pool. I got to meet a lot of cousins, some of whom weren't sure we were related, and I saw a lot of this big country. From Detroit I went to New Jersey, then Indiana, Oregon, Illinois." He looked up and shrugged. "I don't even remember the actual path anymore. It had a lot of twists and turns to it."

Her hand covered his, and the warmth of it was tempting, but he slid his hand away and played with his wineglass.

"The only ones who took any kind of interest in me were the cops," he went on. "Sure, I gave them a reason for that interest. Stealing, fighting, that kind of stuff. And they kicked my butt for that. But then, they kicked my butt when I didn't do anything, either. When I didn't do anything positive, I mean. I don't know why, but they kept on my case, no matter what town I was in."

He stared at the little bit of pale liquid remaining in his glass and drew enough strength from it to go on. "With their pushing, I wound up in the army. Did a little time as an MP. Found my niche in life. Came out and got a degree in criminal justice and now I'm kicking butt to keep kids on the straight and narrow."

It was over, both the past and his recounting of it. Yet Ben needed a little more time to pull the blanket back over the scars. Time to put some peace in his own face. But there was something about her presence that seemed to withdraw everything from him, every last bit of bitterness and anger that needed to be purged from his soul.

"People shouldn't have kids if they can't take care of them," he said.

Seeking the anchor of Jessie's presence, he looked up. Better pity than this feeling of being alone and adrift. "It destroys a kid to know his own mother didn't want him. A kid's whole world is based on a mother's nurturing, and when she doesn't do it, there's no security, no sense of self-worth. Nothing."

Jessie's eyes held more pain than pity, though, and she was obviously groping for words. "You don't know that she didn't want you," she said. "She could have suffered just as much as you."

"She wasn't some helpless victim," he said, but sharing these secret angers with Jessie had somehow made them easier to bear. He took her hands, holding them tightly as if he could will the pain from her eyes. "Hey, everything turned out fine. Just like my old sergeant always told me—it's better being lucky than smart. And I've always been lucky."

Her lips curled into a smile, but Ben knew that her heart wasn't in it. He had never meant to cause her pain in sharing his past with her.

He pulled her to her feet. "They've finally put on some danceable music. Let's get out there and claim some territory."

He led her to the dance floor, then took her into his arms. Just talking to Jessie had laid so many ghosts to rest. Not that they wouldn't surface again, but when they did they'd be more manageable. His demons were no match for her gentleness. He circled her with his arms and pulled her closer to his heart.

God, she was some woman. So full of tenderness, joy and life. He wanted to possess all of her. Hold her to himself for the rest of their natural lives and after, if he could get away with it.

A little voice told him to get out before he got in too deep, but he was a big boy. He could swim no matter how deep, no matter how swift the waters. Besides, Jessie was a big girl. She'd know how to navigate the deep waters as well as he. There wasn't any reason for either of them to run.

Jessie watched the pieces of the night pass them by. A twenty-four-hour drugstore, an oasis of light in the middle of a dark parking lot. A gas station with friends gathered around the pumps as they laughed, safe and happy in the shelter of the overhang. Lovers walking hand in hand, love creating the only glow they cared about.

Jessie looked away, settling her gaze on the dashboard clock in Ben's car. Light and darkness. So much came down to that. The light in Ben's smile, the dark period of her life she'd pushed so far back in her memory. She ought to go on home, but there was nothing there but more darkness.

Jessie closed her eyes. She should have told him everything, about the baby, about the pain. Yet it was a part of her past that she never let herself visit anymore. She'd closed and bolted those doors, and opening them, except on the baby's birthday, was just not done. Better to keep to her ritual than push for Ben's understanding and risk his rejection.

"How about we go back to my house?" Ben asked. "It's a nice night. We can sit outside and count the stars."

"Sure." Perversely she wanted to tell him, and this would give her another chance. Give him a chance to retract those awful words about mothers giving up their kids, to say he understood. She wanted him to hold her in his arms, to reassure her, to ease her troubled thoughts.

They got to Ben's house quicker than she expected. She had no chance to formulate her confession, to plan or practice. Hand in hand, they walked inside. Like those lovers she'd seen, but somehow the glow was muted and hidden. She went to sit on the patio while Ben got each of them a glass of blush wine.

He sat down near her, but she didn't look at him, not at his face anyway. She watched his hand as he reached for hers. Those fingers were perfect—straight and strong. Yet they could be gentle, too, just as his stern, tough exterior hid the gentleness he was capable of expressing. But would that gentleness be there when he knew the truth about her? She pulled her hand away from his and brushed the hair back from her face as she looked up at the stars.

Count the stars, that was what they were supposed to be doing. She started over in the far west, but the sky was too vast to segment and, without segmentation, it was too big to get her arms around. Much too big. Just like her feelings about her daughter.

"How many did you get?" she asked.

She could see Ben frowning at her in the dim moonlight.

"The stars," she said. "You said we were supposed to count them."

He just glanced up at the sky, then back at her. "I'm not done yet."

"Need more time?" she asked.

"Eternity." He put his wineglass off to the side and leaned back, his arm around her shoulders urging her to lean back against him. They shared more of the backyard's vast pool of soothing silence.

"We missed softball practice tonight," he said. "Think they'll still let me play?"

"I think we can talk them into it. Lots of us miss practice because of work. We understand."

"Sounds like the right team for us. I have a feeling tonight wasn't the only late-evening session we may have."

"Probably not."

After that burst, they were caught in the whirlpool of silence, spinning and spinning toward its black vortex of security. It wasn't like they had to talk, Jessie thought. The silence held comfort, too. Comfort that it would be a shame to spoil by spilling more secrets.

She leaned back against him, and the night wrapped itself around her. She could feel his heart beating, feel his awareness of her, and wanted his arms to enclose her and all her fears. She was alone here in the dark with Ben, half lying in his arms with nothing but the night ahead of them. Why was she worrying about the past?

Ben must have felt the same magic, for he turned to embrace her. His hands pressed against her back, holding her closer as his lips pressed softly against her neck and cheek. She could feel his breath drift into her ear, spreading a warm sensation that seemed to blanket her from the summer breeze. They leaned into each other as their lips met in a touch of exquisite tenderness. The night was a friend, smiling at them both.

Their lips moved against each other. Shooting sparks ignited untapped desires, until touching lips wasn't enough. His hands began to roam, weaving a promise of delight in among the strands of hunger. They could dance among the stars and serenade the moon with their joy. They could find in the darkness a flame of light that would burn away loneliness and despair.

Yet even as her own hands couldn't resist caressing his strength, she felt part of her pulling back. She wasn't afraid of making love, yet she wasn't ready to cross that boundary of intimacy, that sharing of the very depths of their being. They were just friends, casual friends, and making love would change that. The ease and comfort they found in each other's company would disappear.

Ben looked into her eyes a long time, seeming to read something there in spite of the darkness. "I think it's time to take you home," he finally said.

"Time to get me back to my car," she corrected.

She clung to him as they walked to his car. Leaned on him once they were inside, eyes closed, and allowed her musings to mingle with the soft balmy breeze as he drove back to her office. She could feel him next to her, sense his eyes on her, and knew the desire that lingered there, but she said nothing. Then she felt the car slow and come to a stop, a sadness weighing on her that the night was over and that somehow she had lost.

"Thanks for everything," she said, though it seemed inadequate.

"Anytime." He opened the car door for her and checked her car out. "You got your keys?"

She held them up along with an attempt at a grin. "Oh, ye of little faith."

He kissed her again then. A quick touch as if he feared more. "I'll follow you home."

She didn't have the energy to argue, though she thought it unnecessary. "Right. See you soon."

She got into her car and pulled out of the lot. She should have told him; she should have found some moment to tell him about her baby. It seemed as though it was a lie, wedging itself between them.

Jessie glanced at her watch as she approached the city limits. Her meeting in North Liberty had lasted a little longer than she'd planned on. It was early for lunch, but it seemed late to head into the office. Instead, she drove on to the West Side Youth Center. A little game of pickup basketball with some of the girls would straighten her out. Exercise, a shower, then a quick bite, and she'd be ready to fight the good fight the rest of the day.

The light turned red. Jessie took advantage of the pause to yawn and massage and stretch her neck muscles. She hadn't slept that well last night. Ben was unsettling, even when he wasn't there.

Should she tell him about her baby or should she keep it her secret? It wasn't as if she had to tell him but, knowing his hurt from his mother's abandonment of him, it seemed dishonest not to.

But was it just fear of his rejection that was holding her back? She was a private person, not used to opening herself up to others. Telling him would expose who she was, what she was. She wasn't certain she could weather his reaction.

After parking her car, Jessie walked briskly into the center. "Hi, Belva," she greeted the black woman in a wheelchair who was manning the desk. "Got any players around?"

"School's out," Belva replied with a smile. "Got a whole passel of them out back."

Cheered by the thought of some physical activity, Jessie quickly changed into T-shirt, shorts and sneakers. Outside, there were two games going on, and she joined the one that had a side short a player. The greetings were brief and terse, enabling Jessie to quickly get into the flow of the game. Within minutes sweat was pouring down her brow and she'd picked up at least three new bruises from some good, solid bumping. She was starting to feel much better.

"Hey, Jess," a girl called out. "We gonna have to lock you out."

"Why?"

"You keep bringing down the law," the girl replied, tilting her head back toward the center building.

Jessie looked back toward where the girl was pointing, and saw Ben approaching. Her heart started working like a yo-yo, bouncing up to the heights of happiness and plunging to the depths of dread.

"I got me a couple of big brothers," another girl whispered at her side. "You want I should have them take care of this guy?"

Jessie's blood pressure settled down to almost normal as she laughed. "Not for now," she replied. "But I'll keep it in mind."

"Hi," Ben said softly.

"Hi, yourself," Jessie replied. She fought the urge to throw herself into his arms.

"Can I join you guys?" he asked.

"We'd need another player besides you for even sides," Jessie answered.

Ben turned to a girl in dark wraparound sunglasses, sitting on the steps. "Want to join us, young lady?"

Instead of replying, the girl just stood up and went inside.

"So much for the old charm," Ben said with a rueful smile.

"Don't worry 'bout it. She don't talk to nobody," one of the girls said.

"Wasn't she here the last time we played?" Ben asked Jessie.

Jessie nodded. "I tried to talk to her the other day. She's not ready to open up."

"Or play ball, apparently," Ben said with a shrug. "It's okay. I'll just sit and watch."

They resumed play again, but it wasn't the same as before. Jessie's play was off, due to the distraction of Ben's presence. The girls snickered and insisted she was hotdogging because her "main dude" was there. When more girls drifted in, Jessie gave up her spot on the court.

"Care for a little stroll by the river to cool off?" Ben asked.

"Sounds great."

She walked down to the river with him, not able to keep from turning back to look for the silent girl in sunglasses. "I don't think that girl's said two words that I've heard."

"When she's ready, she'll talk," Ben said.

"Maybe I should be more forceful when I try to talk to her." They stopped at the river's edge.

"What are you going to do? Racks and dungeons went out with the Middle Ages. Give the kid a chance. Everybody's got secrets and will tell them when the time is right."

Jessie watched the water race by, churned into eddies by the secrets the river bottom held. "What if the time is never right?"

"Then they never get told." He seemed unconcerned about the possibility and sent a stick spinning high in the air to fall in the middle of the river. "There's secrets and then there's secrets. Some things don't ever need to be told, things that carry nothing but pain along with them."

"Like what?"

"Like my mother telling me she hadn't even liked my father very much."

Jessie's heart ached with painful indecision, and she sat down on the sloped bank. Below her, water swirled around a branch half in, half out of the water. The part of the branch below the surface of the water certainly affected how the water moved, but she didn't have to see it, see every scratch or burl on it. Maybe he didn't need to know about the baby. Maybe it was part of who she was but not a part that had to affect her todays.

Ben sank onto the grass next to her, stretching out on the slope. Her eyes strayed to him. He was so strong. Could she find an answer to all her worries in his arms? Or would her problem cease to exist once his embrace erased thought from her mind?

"How'd we get on such a serious subject?" he asked. "I didn't come here to philosophize. I came to apologize."

Jessie blinked. "What for?"

He shrugged. "I came on a little too strong last night."

Heat washed over her with the memories, but it was warm and welcoming. A pleasant dream to hold on to in the nightmarish world she sometimes lived in. She laughed and squeezed his arm.

"I'd be pretty depressed if you didn't. You're one good-looking hunk, Captain Adamanti. And I'm attracted by that and by the gentleman that you are."

"Speaking of being a gentleman," Ben said, and sat up. His voice had lost its laughter.

Jessie looked at him, a fresh crop of worries starting to grow. He looked so serious, when all she wanted was for his lips to play with hers, for his hands to build a fire deep inside her.

"We've had some good times together," Ben went on. "And I sure as hell would like more, but it's only fair to warn you. I learned a long time ago that I'm dedicated to my job. Really dedicated. I just don't have the time or energy for a serious relationship. I'd really like to get to know you better, but I don't want to lead you on, thinking we were heading to a rose-covered cottage behind a white picket fence."

The breeze that blew off the river suddenly seemed sweeter, cooler. "The roses would die anyway," Jessie said. "I'm not too good with plants. I always forget to water them."

"Jessie—"

"No, listen to me," Jessie said. She felt a growing elation, born partly of relief and partly of need. There was so much she worried about that was unimportant. What mattered were things such as how she felt in his arms, how his eyes could light up her soul with laughter and how hungry her body felt when he was near.

"We talked about this before," she said. "Nothing has changed. The kids come first for me and they need an awful lot. I have a great time with you, but I only have so much I can give you, only so much that's left once I take care of the kids."

"So we're good-time buddies," Ben said.

Jessie grimaced. "Like fair-weather friends? How about buddies to make some times good? I have a feeling you're going to be just as good to be around when things go wrong as you'll be when I feel like celebrating."

Ben just looked at her, got to his feet, then pulled her up to him. "That has to be the nicest thing anybody ever said to me. Thank you for the compliment."

After thanking her in words, he let his lips repeat the message by pressing them on hers. The fires of passion were in the background, but muted. This was a touch of friendship, of real caring. Jessie felt at peace in his arms, no longer concerned about the secrets she continued to repress. Voices drifted down from the youth center, breaking the spell, and they pulled apart. Hands joined, they walked back to the center.

"Are you on duty this weekend?" she asked.

"Not officially."

"We don't have a softball game," Jessie said. "I'd like to get away for a day."

"How about the dunes?"

"Sounds great," she replied. "I haven't been there since the fall."

Ben left by the center door. "I've got to get back. Got a staff meeting in twenty minutes."

"Yeah," Jessie agreed. "I'm going to have another go at Miss Sunglasses. I'll give you a call later."

His kiss was quick and hungry, as though he were stealing a chocolate before dinner. Jessie just laughed and watched him go around the side of the building before hurrying back inside herself. This was going to work out great. Loneliness would be a thing of the past. She'd found a kindred soul. Someone who was also dedicated to his job. Someone who didn't want a serious relationship, but enjoyed her company.

It looked as if she were going to have her cake and eat it, too.

Five

"Oh, the weather is just beautiful," Jessie exclaimed as she looked around at the vast canopy of blue sky, shining without a single blemishing cloud.

"Almost as beautiful as you," Ben said. He trailed his fingers down the side of her cheek for a brief shivery moment, then hoisted the cooler to his shoulders.

Jessie picked the blanket out of the trunk and slammed the lid shut. "Are you sure you're not Irish?"

His face darkened suddenly. "I don't know," he said. "For all I know, I could very well be part Irish."

Jessie felt like punching herself. Of all the stupid, thoughtless things to say, that took the cake. "Probably doesn't matter. The Italians have their own version of blarney, so you don't need help from any other ethnic group," she said, trying for lightness.

He'd told her that Adamanti was his mother's name, that his father hadn't even left him a name to live up to. Well, she wouldn't forget it a second time, she vowed, and followed him across the parking lot. He put down the cooler as they got in line at the entrance to the beach.

"I got us some sandwiches from the Submarine Shop," Jessie said. "Lemonade to drink and brownies from the Dainty Maid Shop."

He took her hand in his. "Boy, you are one heck of a cook."

Snatching her free hand back, Jessie pounded him on his shoulder. "I'll have you know I'm a great cook," she insisted. "When I have time, that is." Unfortunately, hitting his rock-hard muscles made her think of other ways of touching them. She pulled her hand back before it could get her into trouble.

"That's right," Ben whispered loudly. "You'd better behave yourself, or I'll tell the rangers on you."

It was their turn at the gate, and a tan-uniformed man gazed impassively at them.

"I had to do it," Jessie told the man. "He's in therapy for a smart mouth, and I have to beat him every time he comes out with a wisecrack."

The ranger didn't answer her, either, concentrating instead on checking the cooler and the folded blanket for any contraband liquor. Finding none, he waved them on.

"Lucky they don't have an ordinance against troublemakers on this beach," she teased.

"Yeah, or you wouldn't be allowed."

They had reached the end of the boardwalk, and Jessie slipped her sandals off, letting her toes play in the sand before kicking some sand at Ben in retaliation.

"We'll see who causes the most trouble," she said.

Being with him was such a joy, her spirit seemed to soar into the heavens. His touch was sweetness itself, but there was so much more to their relationship than that quickness of breath. She could be herself with him, open and honest and—

A little voice from the past reminded her that she wasn't being totally honest with him, but she refused to listen.

"There's a spot near the water," she said, hurrying to a spot ahead.

She spread the blanket out so Ben could put the cooler down. While he stripped off his T-shirt, she slipped out of her cover-up.

Ben looked great in suits and in jeans and old T-shirts, but he was downright dangerous in swimming trunks. His shoulders were broad, his chest a mass of muscles, and below his flat stomach—well, his bikini trunks looked well filled out. She swallowed suddenly as her gaze made its way back up to meet his. The look in his eyes was like that of a pirate eyeing his booty.

"Very nice." His words drifted on his breath, yet she could feel the heat, the intensity behind them. "All that basketball and softball playing has kept you in shape. A very nice shape, I might add."

She wanted his hands to take over where his words had left off. She wanted the wondrous flutter of excitement to last forever. She wanted to feel totally alive, but of course none of that was possible. Not now, not here.

She dropped her wrap onto the blanket even as she turned to race off. "Last one in the water's a rotten egg."

She felt him coming up behind her, felt his gaze scorching her. She reached the water just ahead of him and raced farther in, past her knees and thighs, stopping when it was over her waist. The cooling waves returned her sanity.

"You cheated," Ben said.

She turned to face him, lying back in the water so that it lapped at her shoulders. "I did not. You're just a poor loser."

"Oh, am I?"

He moved closer to her and, though Jessie tried to swim away, he grabbed her ankle. He pulled her close, then his hands ran up her legs and over her thighs to stop at her waist, where they held her prisoner.

"So I'm a poor loser?" he muttered, lifting her feet off the lake bottom.

"One who has to resort to threats, even," she said.

Lifting her up, Ben spun around in the water. But with her stomach pressed against his chest and her legs languishing up against the front of him, it wasn't Ben's movement that was making her dizzy. They were friends, she told herself as she put her hands on his shoulders for balance. Close friends.

"Ready to admit you cheated?" he asked.

Would he put her down then? "Never."

Her hands strayed from his shoulders to his hair, her fingers running through the wet strands. The look in his eyes changed, the fire intensified, and he loosened his hold so that she slipped down in his arms until they were face-to-face. Though the water that swirled around them was cool, their bodies, pressed against each other, seemed hot. The water should sizzle to match the sizzle in Ben's eyes.

"And you said I was the troublemaker," Ben murmured.

His hands moved up over her bare back as she slid her arms around his waist. She could feel his heart racing, its pounding echoed by her own. Time stood still; they were alone, locked in each other's gaze while the rest of the world was shut out.

Suddenly she wanted more from him than friendship. Her body hungered for his completion, for oneness with him. She needed him with an urgency that defied reasoning. The sun seemed only an echo of the heat within her, the pounding rhythm of the waves a weak copy of the pounding of her heart. The fires that had been building within her all week with every touch, every thought of him, were ready to explode into passion.

"Something tells me this isn't the place for what we have in mind," Ben said, his hold on her easing.

"Probably not."

He let her swim away from him, but not too far away. For a time they forced themselves to splash each other like kids, trying to ease the desperate need they each shared. By the time they got out of the water to play a wild game of Frisbee, Jessie's heart was almost back to normal. Lunch calmed it down further, so that when they lay on the blanket side by side to let the rays of the sun warm them, she was relaxed and carefree.

She needed days like this, Jessie told herself as she lay on her back, eyes closed against the sun's brightness. Totally mindless days of relaxation rejuvenated her batteries. They must do the same for Ben, too, for she'd noticed some of the strain lines were disappearing from around his eyes. She should make sure they did this sort of thing more often; it was good for both of them.

Jessie lay still, listening to Ben's even breath at her side. He moved slightly, and the hairs on his arm brushed hers. She suppressed the urge to rub the heat from the spot—or was it to spread the heat?—and rolled over onto her stomach. She opened her eyes to watch him.

There was a slight breeze coming in off the lake. It ruffled the light hairs on his chest, causing them to undulate like a tiny wheat field. Jessie let her fingers cut little furrows in the fluffy mat. She smiled as his muscles twitched involuntarily beneath the feather dance of her fingers.

"Keep that up, and I'm going to do the same thing to you," he warned.

"I don't have any hair on my chest, so there."

"You women never play fair."

"Oh, poor baby." She slid closer, leaned over him and kissed him lightly on the lips. "Speaking of unfair. Look how much stronger you are than me."

She let her fingers dance lightly on his steel-corded shoulders and arms. "You could easily wrap me up in those arms and have your way with me. There would be little that I could do about it."

His eyes devoured her. "Sounds good to me."

"But you're not going to do that."

"Why not?"

"Because you're a gentleman and you're concerned about my needs and feelings, as well as yours."

His hand reached up to caress her upper arm. "And what are your needs and feelings?" he asked.

"They're changing by the moment." Too fast to read almost.

Ben got to his feet, pulling her up with him. "When you figure them out, let me know." His voice was gentle, understanding. "In the meantime, how about a walk around New Buffalo?"

"Play tourist, look in the windows and eat triple-dip ice-cream cones?"

Ben nodded.

"Sounds great to me," she replied. Safer, which was what they both were seeking at the moment.

They packed up the cooler and blanket, then drove south along the lake to the little harbor town. They parked near the beaches and walked east to the business district. Little shops abounded, one with model sailboats, another with paintings on pieces of weathered wood. Ben laughed as hard as she did at the sand sculptures in one window, but had no interest, either, in a T-shirt store.

An ice-cream parlor was in the next block, and they both ordered double-dip chocolate cones. Licking the drips of ice cream, which was melting fast in the heat, they headed back toward the car.

Though their bodies seemed to leap in response to each other, she and Ben had more in common than just shared hungers. More than she had suspected before, adding chocolate ice cream to the list.

"This is getting scary," Jessie said. "Next you'll be telling me pizza with anchovies is your favorite food."

"Anchovies and mushrooms," he corrected.

"Must be the food of workaholics."

"Chocolate and anchovies—what keeps me going," Ben said.

Jessie just laughed and, once she'd finished her cone, slipped her arm through his. She wasn't joking when she said it was getting scary. They seemed so perfect for each other. Now why should that be scary? It ought to make her glad. Maybe because deep down she knew they weren't quite as well matched as it seemed.

Jessie was quiet as they walked along. In the block past the ice-cream parlor, they were refurbishing an old feed mill for more shops. Progress. It brought money and jobs, but it also brought problems. It seemed as though you couldn't have one without the other.

Just like her relationship with Ben. It was great, but it also brought problems, questions that she'd never had to face before.

"Where to now?" Ben asked her as they reached the corner. "More stores? The car and off to elsewhere? Or just home?"

One answer she was sure of was that she didn't want the day to end. "I vote for off to elsewhere, wherever that is."

"Sounds adventuresome." Ben caught sight of a clock in a store window and frowned. "Mind if I call the office? I ought to check in and see how things are."

"No problem," Jessie replied.

They spied a public phone down the block at a gas station and walked over. While Ben made his call, Jessie leaned against a wall, feeling almost sleepy in the cozy heat of the late afternoon. Where should they go from here? Somehow she felt like this was a turning point in their relationship. Crazy as it sounded, it seemed that what they chose to do with the rest of the day would signal where they were headed together. Ben hung up the phone and came over to join her.

"Bad news," he said. "My second-shift duty officer called in sick. I really should go back."

Jessie nodded. "No problem."

"I'm really sorry. We'll come here some other time."

"Hey, I said no problem and I mean it. I know how it is."

While they walked back to the car, Jessie told Ben a story about a little girl she'd placed in a foster home who wouldn't eat unless the family said grace first. She made it light and amusing, so as not to make Ben think she was annoyed that their day was cut short, but inside she wasn't so sure what her feelings were. Was she disappointed or was she relieved?

One thing she was certain of—she had been right when she felt that where they went from New Buffalo would signal where they were going in their relationship. Work had priority, and that made Jessie feel comfortable and safe. That little uneasy feeling in the pit of her stomach was probably just hunger.

Jessie leaned back in a chair in Ben's office, bare feet up on the corner of his desk. She examined the comics one more time, then tossed Saturday's paper aside. Stretching her arms overhead, she watched Ben perusing some reports. A quick trip to a fast-food outlet in the center of town an hour before had silenced their stomachs' growlings, but now other hungers were taking precedence.

Her fingers itched to run through his hair, to straighten those soft curls that hung down on his forehead and to muss up those that lay neatly along the back. She wanted to massage the tension from his shoulders, although maybe her shoulders were where the tension lay. She bit her lip, eyeing the way his fingers held his pen and wishing that they were caressing her instead.

In the past two and a half hours, she'd had a lot of time to think and a lot of time to daydream. While letting work come first for both of them would keep them safe, it didn't mean that they couldn't find other interests to share. Other activities that, for a few moments at least, could come first.

"Not very exciting here," she said.

Shrugging, he pushed his reports aside. "You never know," he said. "Some Saturdays we could use a double shift. And then there are other Saturdays when someone's grandmother could handle the whole thing. That's in addition to running six cards of bingo."

Things could be more exciting elsewhere. Much more. "I bet if you went home, things would run along just fine."

Smiling ruefully, he nodded his head. "Yeah, you're right."

"Well?"

"Jim'll be here in a few minutes, and we can go." He picked up a milk-shake carton, part of Jessie's fast-food foray, and checked its contents. Finding it empty, he threw the refuse in the wastebasket. "Guess I owe you dinner."

"I'm not hungry anymore," Jessie said. Not for food, anyway. "But you do owe me an evening's entertainment."

"Oh." Ben rubbed his chin for a moment. "Want to watch the tractor pulls on cable TV?"

Jessie shook her head, licking her lips.

He looked down at her bare feet on his desk. "Want to stomp some grapes into wine? You're dressed for it."

"You pick the grapes," she replied.

"I don't even know when they're supposed to be picked," he said, frowning.

"Late summer, early fall."

Ben looked at his watch. "We got a little time to kill, then."

Jessie got up to prowl the room restlessly. Stopping behind Ben, she reached her arms down around his neck, running her hands over his chest. "Don't you have a backup identified for your daily duty officer?"

He turned to brush her arm with his lips. "Sure do."

"Why didn't you call him?"

Ben shrugged. "He's got a family. Nice day like today, they probably had something going."

"I'm sure of that," Jessie said. "But I'm also sure that he'd understand if he had to come in."

Ben sat forward, pulling away from her embrace. "I'm sorry I ruined your dinner," he said.

She wasn't going to let him escape behind that wall of gruffness. She sat on the edge of his desk, close enough so that she could brush the hair back from his forehead. It wasn't just her own hungers that were prompting her words; she wasn't that selfish.

"I'm not concerned about that," she told him. "I'm just wondering how your men are going to hone their skills if you're always rushing in and taking over."

He avoided her eyes and just grunted.

She let her fingers glide along the stern line of his jaw, teasing him until she saw him fighting to hold back a smile.

"It's a manager's duty to provide his people with the opportunity to stretch and grow," she pointed out.

"I know."

Neither spoke for a long moment, then Ben leaned back in his chair with a sigh. "You're right. It's not the best thing for my staff if I'm always here to step in. I guess it's just habit." He smiled at her, some of his earlier fire returning to his eyes as he let his hand trail slowly down her bare leg. "I really do appreciate your understanding."

She felt tremors all through her body from his gentle caress. "That's the kind of person I am. Understanding," she said, finding words a chore to think up.

His smile altered to a grin. "Ever have trouble keeping the halo polished?"

She moved away from him before he realized just how much trouble she was having keeping her hands off of him, off of some very private parts of him. "I'm very understanding, especially of someone's dedication to their profession. But you still haven't answered the night's burning question—what do you have planned for the evening's entertainment?"

Frowning, he looked outside the window at the darkening sky. "We'll go to my place."

"And?"

"And I have some wine coolers in the fridge."

She was in a mood to tease. "Sounds delicious."

"They are." He shifted in his seat. "We'll each open a bottle and go out in the backyard."

"And?"

"By then it'll be real dark and the fireflies will be out."

"I always thought it was cruel to catch fireflies."

"We won't catch them," he said. His hand moved to find a slightly different path along her outer thigh. "We'll watch them. Watch how they attract their mates with their lights."

He held her spellbound. A tingle ran down to her toes, as she hung on his suggestion, which was laced with innuendo. "Might pick up some pointers."

"Do we need any?" His voice was soft, yet something in it sent a new wave of awareness through her.

Jessie fixed him with a shy smile. "Sounds like you've got more planned than you're telling."

"Yep." He smiled a moment, a hint of mischief lurking in those sea blue eyes. "We can watch wrestling. It's Saturday night. I'm sure one of the cable channels will have women's wrestling."

"Women's wrestling?"

"So you can pick up some pointers," Ben teased.

Jessie narrowed her eyes. "I'll pick you up," she said in a hoarse whisper. "And give you a triple airplane spin with a body slam."

Ben leaned forward to examine her face, then smiled softly to himself. "I'll be darned. The Michiana Mauler, right?"

"I'm not amused," Jessie replied.

"I could tickle your feet," he said, looking down at her toes. "Would that help your amusement level?"

"I could stomp you—would that help?"

"Time, time," he exclaimed, forming a T with his hands. "This conversation is leading down paths of violence."

Jessie tried not to laugh, not to snuggle down into his arms, but it was a futile effort. Every moment with him was pure happiness. He touched her in ways that she'd never been touched, held her in ways that went beyond embracing. She sat in his lap, wrapping her arms around his waist and laying her head against his chest.

"I'll have you know I'm opposed to violence," he whispered in her ear. "Especially when it's directed toward me."

His voice did terrible things to her equilibrium. She was soaring into the heavens, alone with him and the stars.

"How about we just go to my place?" he said. "Get a couple of those wine coolers, go out in the backyard, lay back on that double chaise longue I got out there and watch the world turn."

"That'll do," Jessie replied with a soft smile. "For a start."

There was a knock at the door, and Jessie slid off his lap in double time, so that she was standing by the time an officer stuck his head in the door. "I'm here, Captain. You can take off if you want."

"Take off what?" Jessie whispered, her voice as soft as a feather's flight.

"Fine, thank you, lieutenant," Ben said, a creeping red tinge in his cheeks the only evidence that he'd heard Jessie.

The door was closed, and Ben gave Jessie a look that was designed to singe her to the core. And as her breathing grew heavier and her heart pounded, she suspected it had. But Ben said nothing. He just got up from the desk and picked her sandals off the floor.

"Want me to carry them or do you want to wear them?"

"I was hoping you'd carry me," she replied. "But the sandals are better than nothing."

He twirled the sandals slowly in his hand as he came closer to her, then swooped her up in his arms. His lips came down on hers in a promise, a vow of joyous delights and insatiable hungers. She was lucky that she wasn't standing, for she didn't think her legs could have supported her. Her breath left, then her reasoning. Ben was her world, her thoughts, her heart. Her arms slid around him, pulling him closer if that were possible. Time had no meaning, then slowly he pulled back from her, though his arms still held her.

"I think it's time to go, don't you?"

"Definitely."

They rode in silence to his house, then walked slowly up to his door. The sidewalk held its warmth from the summery day, and its roughness felt so delicious on the bottoms of her feet. Her soul felt on fire, and the exquisite languor of their movements made the tension all the sweeter.

Ben opened the door and waited for her to go in first. The living room was in shadow and more special that way. She didn't want the harsh lights to awaken reason, to make the evening seem ordinary. This was their night, a time for their hearts and bodies to revel in the others.

Ben followed her inside, and she turned so that they were locked in each other's arms even before he could turn on a light to join the one throwing a pale glow from the hallway. The night promised magic; their embrace promised ecstasy. He crushed her against him, his lips found hers and they were caught up in a wild, pulsating storm. Heart throbbing, gasping breathlessly, she opened her mouth beneath his pressure and felt his tongue against hers.

Warm, moist hungers consumed her. She hadn't felt this way in years. No, she'd never felt this way, never felt that overpowering need to be one with someone else, to have their bodies and souls intertwine. She needed Ben with a desire that went beyond simple physical fulfillment. Her whole body felt red-hot, yet the conflagration was both wonderful and frightening.

His tongue darting and teasing, Ben found a way to pull that knot of tension in her stomach even tighter. She wanted his hands on her, to awaken dreams and blessings that life had not held for her yet. She stirred in his arms, trying to move closer into him, trying to stoke in him the same embers that were alive in her.

"You are so beautiful," Ben whispered, his voice dancing in the air. "You've been driving me crazy wanting to touch you, to hold you."

"I haven't been exactly sane lately myself."

Her hands roamed over his back, but found his shirt a bother. She slid her hands underneath it, feeling the rough, hairy texture of his back. The muscles beneath the surface played under her fingers, danced to the slow, sensual rhythm of her touch.

Jessie felt she was ready to drown in sensations. She was almost too alive, too ready for his touch. Then they both drew back, their eyes locked. She saw hunger and needs in his, but also a gentleness, a wariness born of concern.

"Didn't I promise you a wine cooler?" he asked.

Even though they were apart, his hands seemed unable to leave her. They brushed back her hair, touched her cheek in the softest of caresses. He was giving her time to think, time to breathe, time to change her mind.

"A wine cooler would be great," she said.

He left and she roamed about his living room, not turning on the light, but catching images in the half darkness from the hall light. The room held few knickknacks and no photographs that she could see, but books were everywhere. Mysteries, westerns, classics. A wonderful mixture that was Ben.

"Here you go."

He was back with a wine cooler for each of them. She suddenly didn't want it anymore, didn't want anything but the feel of his hands on her and the delight of resting in his arms. She wasn't certain how to say that, or even if the words would pass her lips, so she sipped slowly at the cool drink in an attempt to douse her inner stirrings.

"Want to go outside?" he asked.

She shrugged. "If you do."

"Not especially."

They were standing in the shadows like two teenagers, holding their drinks and waiting for the other to make a move. She could feel his breath stir her, feel his nearness drawing her like a bee is drawn to the flower. She looked into his eyes. Even in the darkness, she could read their hunger and needs.

"Want that wine cooler?" he asked.

"Not especially."

Her words were so soft she hardly heard them herself, but Ben must have for he took the drink from her hand and put both of them down on a table. She flew back into his arms, to the wild passion that lay in them.

"I guess this means we aren't going to watch the fire-flies," he said.

"You need ideas?" she teased.

His hands had already found their way under her shirt and were sliding over her skin. It had been hot from the sun, then cool from the night, but now it simmered again, reflecting the boiling fevers that lay beneath it.

"I think I've got plenty for tonight," Ben said as his lips came back down on hers.

Their kiss was a wild dance in the moonlight, a celebration of togetherness that would be more magical than ever before. She held him closer, letting him weave a spell around her that she never wanted to leave.

His lips pressed against hers, playing out a love song that his hands sang to her heart. She touched him, loving the feel of his body and loving how he relished her caress. A soft groan escaped his lips, and a sigh slipped from hers. She needed to feel needed, to feel that she alone could bring this desperateness of his to a fever pitch and that she alone could bring him ecstasy.

"Oh, Jess," he whispered, moaned. "Want to go off to elsewhere now?"

"Want to what?" Did his words make sense or was it her mind, too befuddled from his touch to understand?

He swept her into his arms and carried her down the hall, past the intrusive light and into his shadowy bedroom. He laid her down on his bed, and half sat, half lay next to her.

"So this is elsewhere," she murmured.

She couldn't see much of it, but she liked it. She liked the feel of the cool cotton sheet beneath her and the feel of Ben at her side.

He leaned over her, kissing her again and again, but in between, helped her out of her T-shirt and shorts. Her bra came off easily, but her breasts slowed him down. He touched them, touched their softness, until she thought she would lose all reason. When he bent down to let his lips taste their softness, she thought she would die with wanting him.

She pushed at his shirt, tugging it over his head, then helping him get out of his shorts. There was no time for gentle persuasions and coyness. She was liquid fire, raging and ready to devour, and he was pulsating heat.

When they came together, they converged into one with an electrifying force. She hugged him to her, making him her own even as he possessed her and brought her to life. They flew like shooting stars into the heavens, but all the while bound together, holding on to each other as if nothing could ever break them apart.

Then the fires exploded and died down. Smoldering embers took their place, and sweet warmth took the place of white heat. Jessie smiled, a sigh shuddering through her body as she closed her eyes and rested her head against Ben's shoulder.

* * *

"My, my," Jessie exclaimed the next morning. "Eggs Benedict. Who made it?"

She was wearing one of Ben's T-shirts, sitting down at his patio table, eyes glowing in anticipation of breakfast.

"I did," he said with a chuckle.

The look she gave him was not at all trusting and believing. "Right."

"I did. While you were sleeping, I drove over to the grocery store for the ingredients. A special lady deserves a special breakfast."

"Oh." She cut off a neat little pile, being sure to include all the ingredients, for her first bite.

The uncertainty in her eyes was from the situation, he knew, not the meal, but he would chase away whatever shadows lurked in her heart. If eggs Benedict did it, fine. If it took a few more kisses, all the better.

"Not bad," she said as she tasted it.

"Not bad?" He cut a piece for himself. "I would say more like excellent."

"You're much too modest," she said, taking another bite.

"I always thought it was more important to be honest than modest."

Jessie gave him a crooked smile before continuing with breakfast. Ben wasn't eating too fast himself, though; he couldn't help but watch her. Her hair was tied back and she didn't have a single bit of makeup on, but she was so beautiful, it was almost breathtaking. Jessie looked fresh, young, and . . . innocent.

A smile of wonder sneaked onto his face as memories of last night strolled through his mind. *Innocent* was not a word he would have thought of last night. Yet *fresh* would certainly have fit. He shook his head slightly. Jessie was an unbelievable combination of angel and woman.

"Care for anything else?" he asked as Jessie pushed her plate away.

"No, thank you. I hardly ever have breakfast, so this was quite a change."

"You should always eat breakfast," he scolded.

"I don't always have time."

"That's no excuse." She needed to take better care of herself. Maybe she needed him to help take care of her.

She made a slight face at him. "Fine, I'll hire a maid."

"Butlers work just as well," he assured her.

"I'm sure they're just as expensive," she replied.

"Some of them." He pushed his own plate aside. "Although, I understand that such services can be obtained for a very reasonable, and I might add modest, price."

She lifted one eyebrow. "Oh?"

"Absolutely." He reached over to take her hand, keeping his touch gentle. "In fact, some of these very talented men are merely interested in a little affection."

"Are they, now? I'll have to keep that in mind." The smile she gave him was full of radiance, more than enough competition for the midmorning sun now warming his patio, but she pulled her hand away. Standing up, she stretched, both arms over her head, so that his T-shirt did nothing to hide her womanly curves. He tasted his hunger for her again.

"I should be getting home soon," she said, gathering the breakfast dishes together.

"It's still early." He didn't really want her to go. Living with dark clouds as long as he had, he was very skittish about letting go of the sunshine.

"The Captain's been alone for almost twenty-four hours," she said. "That's really not fair to him. He has plenty of dry food, but by now he'll be getting lonely."

When you leave, I'm going to be lonely, Ben thought. "Maybe you should get him a buddy. Someone to stay with him all day."

She nodded. "I've thought of getting another cat. But Captain Kidd isn't a youngster anymore. I don't know how he'd adjust to a newcomer."

Captain Kidd wasn't the only one. "You'll never know until you try."

Jessie just nodded.

They'd tried a lot. Tried being friends, then companions and now lovers. Sure, there'd been a risk each time they took another step forward, but now that he knew Jessie, he knew how empty his life had been.

"I really should be getting home," she said again, as if she were trying to convince herself more than him.

He stood up and took the plates from her. "I'll take care of this. You go get dressed."

He took one last look at Jessie as she glided back into his house. Perfect. She was just perfect.

Six

"There's a cold front moving in," the radio announcer said cheerfully. "Fifty percent chance of thundershowers today, and fifty percent chance for tonight."

Jessie sighed as she looked up at the overcast sky. It had been so beautiful this weekend, and now look at it. Dark, gloomy clouds full of moisture. Well, it suited her mood.

Saturday had been great and Saturday night had been simply marvelous, but Sunday had brought the hard edge of reality back into her life. By the early afternoon Jessie was well on her way to a serious case of mopes. One night with the man, and she couldn't get him out of her mind! What kind of independence was that? By evening she was snapping at her cat and refusing to answer her phone.

Ben had called. Actually he'd called three times. Once around four, leaving a message that he would like to take her to dinner. Then he called at seven, saying to give him a call if she wanted to go for a walk and an ice-cream cone. His last call was a little after eleven, wishing her pleasant dreams.

One part of her itched to snatch up the receiver each time she heard his voice, but another part hesitated. She wanted to talk to Ben, walk with him, hold hands, hug and be hugged. She wanted to love him every which way possible. Yet she held back, wondering what she had gotten herself into. Wondering what she had left herself open for now that she had let down her defenses. Had she left herself vulnerable? Would she pay in sorrow and bitterness for a night of pleasure and contentment?

Jessie pulled into her parking place and vigorously pulled up the hand brake. Dummy. She certainly had shown how independent she was—eating cold cereal for dinner while moping about Ben instead of sharing an anchovies-and-mushroom pizza with him.

"Either be really independent or be a clinging vine," she told herself as she got out of the car. "But make up your mind!"

She slammed the car door, took one step and stopped. A sinking feeling dropped her stomach down to her toes. Gritting her teeth, she turned to look into her car. Her car keys were hanging brazenly from the ignition.

"Damn," she exploded. "Damn, damn, damn."

Pausing to give the dark skies above her one of the fiercest glares she could muster, Jessie stomped on into her office.

"Hi, Jess," Marla said. "You got some messages."

There were two messages. One from Ben, just saying he'd called. The please-return-call box had been checked. Probably nothing urgent. Most likely not even business.

She made herself look at the other message. It was from a Mrs. Belanger and it was marked urgent. Sammy had run away again. Great.

Hurrying to her desk, Jessie grabbed the phone and dialed the woman.

"What happened this time?" Jessie asked.

"I needed to go to the store for a few things," Mrs. Belanger told her. "I asked him to keep an eye on his little brothers. And he just up and stomped out of the house. Yelling at me. Saying he wasn't no baby-sitter. Said I should go out and hire some girl. It was only gonna be a few minutes, Miss Jessie. Just a few minutes."

Jessie sighed. The odds were high that Sammy would come home. He'd run away before and had always come back. Problem was, the kid usually got into trouble during his excursions. He almost always took the opportunity to steal. Do a little shoplifting.

"He'll come back, Mrs. Belanger," Jessie said. "He always does."

"Yeah, I suppose you're right."

"I'll call if I hear anything," Jessie said. "I want you to do the same, please."

The woman agreed and, after a few more consoling words, Jessie hung up. For a moment she sat there, tapping her fingers on the desk. She could really use a good dose of Captain Ben Adamanti about now. He would know how to banish the storm clouds from her day, but did she dare? Ben's telephone message sat in front of her, and she stared at it. She reached for the phone.

The day really had an ominous feeling to it. What else would happen? It was said that bad news came in groups of three, and she'd already locked her keys in the car and found out about Sammy. She pulled her hand back.

Maybe it would be better not to call him. She doubted that he had any bad news for her, but why tempt fate?

No sooner had she made that decision than her phone rang. It was the director of the West Side Youth Center.

"Hi, Harry. How is it going?"

"Pretty near to horrible," he replied. "The city's cutting our funding in half for next year. We're going to have to do some serious fund-raising."

"I'm not much good at that," Jessie said.

"Me, either," Harry said. "I'm trying to line up some movers and shakers with deep pockets. You get any names, pass them on to me."

After hanging up, Jessie dropped her chin into her hands. Great, just great. Everything was turning to ashes.

Her glance strayed back toward Ben's note. The youth center was the third piece of bad news. It was safe to call Ben now.

Jessie reached for the phone, yet hesitated. There weren't any guarantees that a call to Ben would turn out well. Might just start another group of three. She resolutely turned herself to the pile of correspondence in front of her. It really was that kind of day.

Jessie got the call that Sammy Belanger was picked up for shoplifting right after lunch and, using the extra set of car keys in her desk, drove over to the police station.

"Go on back to Ben's office," the dispatcher told her.

Jessie gave the woman a weak smile as she went down the hall. Somehow this wasn't what she'd have picked for their first meeting after making love. How was she to act when encountering her lover in a business situation? Did she pretend they'd never met, that they were close friends? Miss Manners hadn't covered this subject in great enough detail.

Jessie gave a quick knock on the office door and opened it. She didn't need Miss Manners's advice after all. It was obvious from Ben's dark scowl that their weekend had had no effect on him at all. No positive effect, that is. He wasn't going to listen to her views any more carefully, or give any greater consideration to them than before. Sammy Belanger was sitting near the door, fear written all over his face. Apparently Ben was playing good-cop/bad-cop all by himself.

"Hi, Sammy," Jessie said softly.

The boy darted a glance her way and nodded once.

Jessie gave him a smile before turning to Ben. "Captain Adamanti," she said. She kept her eyes as cool and distant as possible, playing his game, too.

"Miss Taylor," he replied.

"Why did you call me?" Jessie asked. Her voice sounded a tad too brusque even to her ears, but she wasn't in the mood for cajoling. With all that needed attention in his department, Ben had other things to do besides bullying kids. Unless this was just his way of letting her know that the weekend hadn't meant anything to him. That thought brought surprising pain along with it, but she closed her heart to it all.

"Why didn't you call Sammy's mother and release him to her custody?" Jessie asked.

"I'm not releasing Sammy."

"What?" Jessie could feel the flames of anger start in her stomach and spread up into her neck and cheeks. What kind of game was he playing? She took a deep breath to calm her voice and turned to Sammy. "Why don't you wait for me out in the lounge?"

The boy quietly rose and went to the door.

"And don't take off," Ben ordered. "If you do, I'll find you no matter where you go."

Jessie saw a spark of anger in the boy's eyes, but he said nothing and shut the door as he left.

"Was that really necessary?" Jessie snapped.

"I just didn't want him to get any ideas."

"So you have to scare him half to death?"

"Oh, come off it," Ben snapped back. "That's a street kid you're talking about."

"That doesn't make him any less human."

"No," he replied hotly. "But it does mean he's got a hell of a lot more backbone than you bleeding-heart social workers give him credit for."

They traded glares. There'd been so much sharing right here in this very office. Sharing of compassion and tenderness, of dreams and joys. Jessie had thought from those things would come respect. Apparently she had been wrong.

Ben Adamanti could be very pleasant and charming when what he wanted couldn't be bludgeoned out of a person, but when he didn't need the charm, he went back to the iron fist. The same old knot-head he'd always been.

"Jessie, won't you sit down, please?"

A bitter smile twisted her lips. "Why? Don't you like looking up to someone when you talk?"

She could see the muscles in his temples twitch. He was furious, but she didn't care—so was she. Angry and hurt, and the more she fought back, the less she could feel her pain, the less he would be able to suspect it existed.

"Maybe you should have your adult visitors stand more often," she said. "Then you'll have a better idea of what it's like to be a child, where everyone in authority towers over you."

"I don't think we're going to get anywhere until you sit down."

"You mean you're not going to do anything until I sit down."

Ben just looked down at his hands. She would have liked to play his game, show him she was just as tough and stubborn as he was, but indulging in childish whims would just hurt Sammy's case. She sat down.

"Why aren't you releasing him to his mother?" she asked.

"Jessie, this is the third time the kid's been picked up for shoplifting."

"It's just his way of crying for help."

"Well, maybe he'd better increase his vocabulary. It's obvious he's not getting the help he needs."

They were back to trading glares. Jessie clenched her fists in her lap, feeling alternately like striking out or crying. As the seconds ticked off, she let her temper grow to overpower the hurt. She was exasperated at the two of them. At Ben for making her care, then showing her he didn't. And at herself for being so weak. All their new relationship did was head her to disappointment.

"Jessie," he said. "We have a long afternoon ahead of us."

"So maybe we ought to get started."

They began with calls to the juvenile judge and the county prosecutor, then more calls to the Boys' Training School, to the school guidance counselor, and to Sammy's mother.

As he talked on the phone, Ben pounded his fist and said releasing Sammy to his mother's care wasn't going to work. He'd just steal again. Then Jessie would take the phone and cajole and negotiate. She pointed out that Sammy had never physically harmed anybody. He was a bright boy. And on top of everything, the Boys' Training School was filled, loaded to forty percent over capacity.

She and Ben didn't exactly raise their voices to each other again, though neither did they talk more than necessary. But more than once, Jessie caught herself watching him, watching his hands as he pounded them to make a point or tapped with impatience on the desktop. She remembered how alive those hands had made her feel, how safe she'd thought she'd been when he held her, and her anger flared back. When she had stupidly trusted Randy years ago, she had been a child. What excuse did she have for trusting Ben?

By late afternoon Sammy's case was finally resolved. He would be sent to the Family and Children's Service Center, where he'd be in residential facilities for a month then would go into outpatient counseling.

After the last call was made, Jessie fell back exhausted. She could hear the scratching of Ben's pen as he filled out some forms, but then that stopped and the silence in the room grew deafening. She should leave, she told herself. They had nothing more to say to each other, but she couldn't make her feet move.

"I care about those kids just as much as you do," he finally said.

Jessie gave him a quick glance and found his eyes had lost their hardness. The ice had melted into a deep, dark sea that held warmth and something else. Worry? She wasn't sure how to deal with that, so she began to pick up her papers.

"I just show it in different ways."

Very different, but she didn't want an argument, so she settled on a single grunt.

"Have you tried getting Sammy into counseling before?"

"Yes."

"Have you succeeded?"

She clenched her teeth a moment. "No."

"You get all kinds of excuses, right? They're all filled. There's a waiting list longer than your arm. He doesn't qualify."

It was safest just to nod.

"Well, my big mouth shook the wheels up. After I dragged them through the grinder, they realized there'd be more than his mother on their case the next time the kid stole or broke some other law."

All right, so he had a point. She wasn't going to give in so easily. "You'd still be pounding the desk if I hadn't negotiated a way to save face and still help the kid."

He leaned back in his chair, a broad smile erasing any last traces of scowl that still lingered in the air. "Good-cop/bad-cop."

Some of her vehemence returned, but with a different focus. "You mean that's all this was—some stupid role-playing game?"

"It was a way of getting the job done."

"Damn it anyway," Jessie cried out, throwing her papers back onto his desk. "All that scowling and snarling was just part of some stupid role? How the hell was I supposed to know that?"

"Well, I—"

"You act like you hate my guts, but I'm supposed to understand it was all an act?"

"Jessie, Jessie, Jessie."

Ben was around his desk in an instant, taking her into his arms. The tempest died down with his touch until what was left was the memory of the pleasure his arms held, the need to feel that pleasure again.

"You should know I wouldn't ever hurt you," he whispered, his lips brushing hers in a plea for forgiveness.

"How would I know that?" she asked. His eyes said wonderful things to her, melting her worries and allowing that slow fire to smolder inside her. "You were awfully convincing," she added.

A slight shadow crossed Ben's face. "Well, it wasn't all an act. Why didn't you return my calls?"

Jessie sighed. "Because I wanted to so badly."

"Want to run that past me again?"

"Because I'm not getting involved, and every time you called, I forgot that. I forgot how independent I was and how I didn't need anybody else. The only way to keep my heart in line was to ignore your calls."

He tightened his hold on her. "Maybe if you hadn't, you would have known I wasn't mad at you this afternoon."

"Maybe."

"Maybe nothing," he argued. "You have to understand, Jess, that needing each other doesn't mean we aren't independent. I need you to talk to, to laugh with, and a few other ways that I probably can't demonstrate right here."

His gaze was fiery, and she just laughed and cuddled closer into his embrace.

"But that doesn't mean that I'm not independent. It means that I have a friend I cherish. A friend whom I work wonderfully well with."

"We do make a hell of a team," Jessie admitted.

"We sure do," he quietly agreed. "In a lot of ways."

The kiss she'd been waiting for, wanting and needing, came then. His lips brought peace and pleasure to her soul, a serenity that felt like warm sunshine. She had been frightened, but Ben's touch banished any fears, banished even the memory of them.

But then his touch changed, or her reaction to it did. The warmth of sunshine began to smolder, and peace became overshadowed with hunger. Her body remembered Ben's feel, his scent and the wild ecstasy he'd given her, and wanted it again. His kiss wasn't enough; she needed to feel more—much more.

They pulled apart, staring at each other with hunger in their eyes. She held his hand for a brief moment, then let go to pick up her papers. "I'll take Sammy to the center," she said. "We can drop by his house and pick up a few things first."

"Thanks," he replied. "It looks like all of my people are tied up."

He touched her, his hand sliding slowly along her cheek. Shivers of desire ran down her spine.

"I'm not going to make softball practice. I've got a meeting tonight," he said. "A countywide task force on youth gangs."

"We may not even have practice. Depends on the weather."

"Sorry we can't have dinner together."

"Yep."

"I'll pick you up tomorrow morning. You need breakfast more than anything."

She tried giving him another glare, but it turned into a smile. "You always have to do things your way, don't you?"

"Only if it's good for you."

Jessie snorted. "And who decides that?"

"You do," he said, kissing her once more, but with lightning quickness. "You just know I'm good for you."

Ben paused outside the seminar room and massaged the back of his neck. These meetings were a pain. Youth cops from all over the county, with a couple of academic experts thrown in for seasoning. And everyone had to put their two cents in.

He took a deep breath before plunging into the stream of university students pouring out of their night-school classes. After three hours of discussion, everyone agreed that they desperately required more money and people, and also agreed they weren't going to get either. He shook his head. Blessed are the wheels, for they shall spin in circles.

This would have been an evening much better spent with Jessie. Teasing her gently about this afternoon and loving her maybe not so gently. For the moment he was lost in the memory of her smile, the soft laughter that her eyes held and the sweet fragrance of her hair. Then some jerk bumped into him and broke into his dream.

Damn. Now that he had somebody to spend his off-hours with, nonproductive meetings like this seemed an even worse waste of time.

Ben paused at the top of the stairs. He was starving. Should he go over to Stude's or down to the lounge for a couple of candy bars? Stude's didn't seem too appealing alone, though he'd been there on his own most of the time. He must not be that hungry. He took the stairs two at a time.

It wasn't that he had to have Jessie with him everywhere he went. He just wasn't in the mood for Stude's tonight. He stopped in front of the candy machine. Who filled these things anyway? He wanted something with peanuts, lots of peanuts, not this solid sugar stuff. Glaring didn't change the contents, though.

"Ben? Don't tell me that the great Ben Adamanti is going to put white sugar into that beautiful, healthy body of his."

Oh, hell. It couldn't be. Although Ben could feel a stiffness in his neck, he slowly turned his head. Damn. It was.

"Hi, LeAnn."

His ex-wife still had her long slender body and, judging from the gleam in her eye, her mean sense of humor.

"You're looking good, Ben." Her fingers quickly brushed at his hair. "Getting some gray in the locks, but that's better than bald any day. I think bald men are so ugly, don't you?"

"I've never concerned myself with how other men look."

She laughed and patted his cheek. "Still quick on the uptake. Haven't lost too much to the years yet."

"Thanks," he murmured. "I guess."

"So what are you doing here?" LeAnn asked. "Going to school?"

Ben shook his head. "Gang Task Force meeting for the county."

"Oh." She made a face. "Still playing cops and robbers. Aren't you tired of that kind of stuff yet?"

"Not yet," he replied. "Are you taking a class?"

LeAnn nodded. "Yeah. I'm going for my realtor's license. There's good money in that."

"Isn't your husband making enough? I thought he was a CPA or something."

Laughing loudly, LeAnn shook her head. "You cops are so naive. Don't you know you can never have enough? Besides, we have some kids now, twin girls. And they eat up money like it's going out of style."

"I presume you had them because you wanted to."

This time it was LeAnn's turn to shrug. "Pretty much."

Neither had anything else to say, but then they never did have much to talk about. The silence was stretching on to awkward when Ben forced a smile to his face.

"Well, I gotta run. Nice seeing you again, LeAnn."

"Yeah, same here. I'll keep an eye out. Next time maybe we can go out and have a brew. You know, for old times' sake."

"Sure."

Ben hurried down the hall to the parking lot. He'd sure keep an eye out, too. That way, he could run before she saw him.

Exiting the parking lot, Ben headed toward Lincoln Way and its string of fast-food outlets, but by the time he'd reached them he was in a blue funk and not hungry anymore.

It wasn't exactly LeAnn, though she always seemed to sour everything when she was around. It was probably a combination of everything—no dinner, boring meeting and then her. He just needed to go on home.

He turned the car around and headed back toward home. No, what he needed was to see someone who could make the sun shine.

He turned north and took a pass by Jessie's apartment. He drove slowly, letting his patrolman's eye scan the area. Everything looked in order. She'd said that she had some work to do tonight. Judging from the light in her window, she was doing it at home. Maybe she could use a little help. He parked the car.

"Yes." Her voice answering his ring was tentative.

"Hi," he said. "It's Ben. Did you put out a lady-in-distress call?"

"No."

"Are you sure? I'm positive there was somebody at this address who was lonesome and blue."

"Sounds like I had my radio up too high and you tuned into a country-and-western song."

Talk about blues—his were disappearing faster than the speed of light. "Maybe I ought to come up and check your place out anyway. As long as I'm here."

"Well, as long as you're here." She tried to sound resigned, but couldn't hide the hints of laughter.

She buzzed him in, waiting for him at the doorway. The night was warm, and she was wearing just a T-shirt and short shorts. Oh, my. Very nice short shorts that allowed him a good view of some very nice legs.

Ben stepped inside only to be greeted by a mangy-looking feline. "That's Captain Kidd?"

"Yep," she replied. "Captain, this is Captain Adamanti."

Captain Kidd grumbled. "No, he doesn't outrank you," she assured the cat.

Ben pulled out his identification. "See, I'm a police officer. I'm safe to let in."

The cat growled.

"He's not impressed," Jessie said, laughing.

She guided him past the suspicious animal and to the sofa. Various booklets were strewn in front of it. Captain Kidd, still complaining, made his way after them into the living room.

"Did I disturb something?" Ben asked as they sat down.

"The youth center funding has been cut," Jessie replied. "I'm checking board members from other organizations that might be willing to help us."

"Must be something in the air," he said. "I'm looking for some angels myself."

"Funding cuts in your department?" she asked in surprise.

"Actually a more personal angel. It wasn't a great night."

The tension was still in his shoulders, and Jessie was so close. She must have recently showered; there was such a sweet clean smell about her. No colognes, no makeup, just pure Jessie.

He leaned to his side, laying his head in that sweet spot between her shoulder and her breasts. His eyes closed. She smelled even better up close. Her fingers, so cool, began lightly massaging his neck.

"You look tired," she said.

"A little bit."

She massaged his shoulders. "Meeting not very exciting?"

"Oh, pretty usual, I guess. A lot of talk, no progress because there's no money."

"Sounds typical."

"Yeah." Lord, her fingers could work magic. His tension fled and sweet peace took its place. "Then when I was leaving, I met my ex-wife."

"Oh?"

"Still the same old reaction."

Jessie's fingers slowed. "You missed her?"

He looked up into her eyes and laughed. "No. Relieved that I didn't have to go home to her."

"Oh."

Her one syllable said volumes, though, and what it omitted, her fingers spelled out for him. That sweet peace he'd been enjoying took its turn at ebbing away, but the tension that came instead was a far cry from his tension when he'd arrived. It was a deep, burning need to hold a certain woman in his arms, to make her his own in the most basic of ways.

Jessie's massage turned into a series of caresses. Her fingers worked a magic that made any weariness fade away. He felt alive and strong, a fire running through his veins that needed to consume all.

"You know, I was thinking," Jessie said softly. Her breath stirred the hair on the back of his neck. "Since your evening was so rough, maybe you shouldn't drive anymore tonight."

He turned to look up into her warm eyes. "I was thinking that same thing myself.

"Oh, were you?"

Her eyes teased him, but when he got to his feet and swept her into his arms, her gaze changed. The light laughter was gone, vanished in the face of his hunger as her own fires leapt up to join his. They didn't need words or wine, just each other, and their need was great enough to make the rest of the world disappear.

He carried her into her bedroom and in the semidarkness undressed her. Her skin was so smooth, so soft and warm that he couldn't touch her enough. His hands slid over her flat stomach to cup her breasts, but then his hands weren't sufficient and his lips needed to taste her freshness.

His mouth tugged at her breasts, then left a trail of kisses along the side of her neck. He found just the right spot to make her shiver with delight; the more he caressed it with his tongue, the more she curled into him. His needs grew, but his hands couldn't be still. Down her sides they roamed, cupping her firm buttocks and pressing her into him.

There was warmth about her, a gentleness that was so alien to his roughness that he wanted to devour her. He needed to capture her essence, to imprison her soul inside him so that he could possess her totally. Touching was only a beginning; possession was what he craved.

Jessie moaned softly under his touch, her body shivering in response. She touched him all over with her hands, bringing him to the brink of ecstasy. Over and over her fingers teased him, making him hotter and more desperate, then suddenly she shifted her position and took him inside her. Moving beneath him, she was everything. She was everywhere. He couldn't breathe; he couldn't think. There was just Jessie and her love, making his world magic.

She came to life along with him, clinging to him as they were both catapulted to the edge of the precipice. Then they lay together, their breathing easier, their pulse rates slowing from their frantic race.

"Ah, Jess," he murmured as he pulled her closer into his arms to rest.

She snuggled against his chest and, from the even rise and fall of her breasts, he knew she'd fallen asleep. Holding her like this was just as special as loving her.

Seven

"Here she comes!"

"Hurry up, Jess!"

"Come on. We're starving!"

Jessie had never been greeted so effusively by the kids from the youth center, and thought it might have something to do with the huge box of hot-dog buns she was carrying.

"Boy, glad you finally got here," Ben said from behind the grill he was manning. "Thought they were going to tear me from limb to limb."

"And you couldn't fight off these sweet little kids? You must be getting old." Jessie ripped open the box and began to hand him buns to fill.

"Them's fightin' words, lady," Ben said. "Just you wait until tonight, and we'll see who's getting old."

He leaned over when reaching for the next bun to plant a kiss on her lips. It was quick as a summer storm, but it packed a mighty wallop that she felt all the way down to her toes.

"Ooh, kissee, kissee," one of the kids cried, and the others started giggling.

"Better watch it or you'll go to the end of the hot-dog line," Ben warned, but his threat only ignited more laughter.

When he turned and found Jessie was laughing, too, he stopped filling the hot-dog buns and frowned at them all. "I'd like a little respect around here," he growled.

"That's what you're getting," Jessie pointed out, and shoved a hot-dog bun into his hands. "A little respect. Very little."

Ben retaliated in typical Ben fashion, which meant a totally unexpected way. He tossed the hot-dog bun into the air and swooped Jessie into his arms.

His lips met hers like a marauding pirate, ready to plunder and pillage. First they took her sense of propriety, then her ability to think clearly and finally her common sense. Once that was done, her defenses overrun and her heart waving a white flag of surrender, his mouth began a second attack.

This time it was a slow, seductive assault. The warm crush of his body awoke delicious memories, as well as the embers of passion. Lazy little flames of desire licked at her, turning her limp, without resistance to the sensual pressure of his lips. When he let her go, the kids applauded.

"Boy, I don't think my mom ever got kissed like that," one girl said.

"I thought they just did that in the movies," another said.

"I'm hungry," someone else announced, and the mood was broken.

At least among the kids it was. Ben gave her a sidelong look, his eyes clearly smoky. "I'm hungry, too," he whispered.

Jessie just gave him a mocking glance and doubled the pace of her serving chores. "You shouldn't start what you can't finish," she pointed out in her best scolding tones, though they just covered up the same yearnings.

"Who says I can't finish?" he said. "Is that a dare? Come a little closer, lady, and I'll show you that I can too finish."

Jessie just laughed, her heart too full of joy not to let it spill over. Life had never been so sweet or so satisfying as it was now. Ben was like a spice that gave everything zest. She was doing the same things she'd always done, but somehow it was better, richer. She wanted to hug the world.

"You guys need a break?" the director of the youth center asked, coming over to the grill. "You work with these critters all week—we don't want to tire you out on your day off."

"Hey, no problem," Ben assured him. "It keeps us off the streets and out of the bars. And you know how Jessie is. If she doesn't have something to occupy herself, she'll just start trouble."

"Thanks a lot," Jessie said, but she knew, even though Ben was teasing, that there was an element of truth in what he said. Not the part about the streets and the bars, but needing something to occupy herself. She needed to give herself to others, and the kids here ached for the attention. They were like one big family.

"Get yourselves something to eat and relax," the director ordered, taking the long barbecue tongs from Ben. "Got a big softball game at two."

Ben grabbed a hot dog for each of them, while Jessie got two glasses of lemonade, and they wandered among the kids. Girls called out teasing comments, boys half-challenging ones, but all around her, Jessie felt acceptance and caring. Even the sun was like a friend today, smiling down a pleasant summer warmth on them all.

"Sometimes it feels like they're all my family," Jessie said.

"Yeah, I know what you mean." Ben finished his hot dog and put his free arm around her shoulder. "They're kind of all my kids. That's why I come down hard on them, because I don't want them to screw up their lives."

She believed that about him now, though at one time she hadn't. He cared just as deeply as she did, but he showed it differently. Maybe it was like her mother and father. Mom always had been the one to comfort; Dad demanded responsibility, but they both loved their children in their own ways. Just as she and Ben cared in their individual ways. It was just further proof that they were perfectly suited.

"That kid must be stowing it away for the rest of the summer," Ben said.

Jessie followed his gaze and saw the young teenage girl with the wraparound sunglasses. She had a plate on her knees, piled to overflowing with food, but not just the ever-popular cake and cookies. She had fried chicken, ribs and french fries. Fairly substantial food.

"Does anyone know who she is?" Ben asked.

"No." Jessie shook her head. "She doesn't talk much to anybody. Not even the other girls. I've tried a couple of times, but she always walks away."

"Why don't you give it a try now?"

Jessie sighed, discouragement welling up in her, coupled with pain she felt for the child. "She'll just walk away again. Maybe there's something about me that strikes her wrong."

Ben just chuckled. "With that plate full of food she's juggling, I'm not sure she can just up and scamper off."

Jessie felt a glimmer of hope grow in her. "You're right." Maybe this time she could get somewhere.

They moved closer to the girl, who seemed to be ignoring them. Jessie sat down next to her.

"Hi," Jessie said. "Remember me? My name is Jessie Taylor."

No response.

"I'm a social worker. I'm here a lot around noon. Usually I'm playing basketball with the girls."

Still no answer.

"I don't just play basketball, though," Jessie said. "I help the girls with their problems, too. You know, with school. Jobs, if they need money. If they get in trouble with the police. That kind of thing."

She just sat there while the girl shoveled food in her mouth. Ben was right. It looked as if the kid was figuring on no tomorrow. Jessie hurt for her, but unless the girl gave her some information, there was no way she could help. Jessie looked up at Ben. He gave her a smile that said to keep trying.

"What's your name?" Jessie asked.

"Maggie."

Jessie blinked in surprise. "Well, I'm very pleased to meet you, Maggie," Jessie said. "Do you live around here?"

Apparently one answer was Maggie's limit. She was back to eating with her full concentration.

"Well, I'm glad you come here," Jessie told her. "There are lots of people here who care about kids and are willing to help in any way they can. If you're having troubles or just want to talk, let one of us know."

The girl said nothing more, didn't even look Jessie's away. So Jessie just reached into the pocket of her shorts for one of the business cards.

"Here's my telephone number. If you ever need me, just call."

Maggie didn't take the card, so Jessie stuck it in the pocket of the girl's T-shirt. She'd probably just throw it away, but it was worth a try. Jessie got up and gave Ben her hand, needing his strength for just a moment.

"Good job," Ben murmured after they'd walked some distance from Maggie.

"Thanks." But her gloom demons seasoned her voice.

Ben pulled her to a stop and put his arms around her shoulders. "Hey, I mean that," he said.

Jessie just grunted. "The kid obviously needs help. What good does knowing her first name do?"

"Jess. She hasn't talked to anyone else, has she?"

"No."

"Well, a journey of a thousand miles starts with a single step. Or a single word."

She couldn't think of a snappy answer to that cliché, so she just wrapped her arms around his waist and pulled herself close.

"The kids sense you really care for them. Hell, anybody can see that. So they trust you. Believe me, you've made headway today. I'd bet the family farm on it."

"I hope so."

She wanted so desperately to help, but hearing Ben say she'd done some good would make it all complete. The realization shook her. Kids required approval from adults they cared about—adults didn't. Especially not independent adults like herself.

She let go of Ben, her heart troubled. Nearby was the dessert table with a line of kids waiting for cake.

"I think maybe they could use some help over there," Jessie said, and without waiting to see if he followed her, she hurried over.

Jessie picked up a knife and began cutting a huge sheet cake that had been donated to the youth center's picnic. Ben was at her side, sliding the pieces onto plates as she cut them. They were a great team, she told herself. Working together with kids professionally and voluntarily, right down to serving hot dogs or cake. And making love. Her cheeks flared with color at the thought.

Everything they did, they did naturally complementing each other. Even without words, they knew where the other was, what the other was thinking. Knowing what the other one needed. It wasn't as though they were friends; it was as though they were in love.

The ground seemed to shake beneath her, though Jessie knew she was the only one who'd felt it. Love? She couldn't be in love with Ben. She had vowed never to love again. Love had destroyed her, had ripped apart her life and left her in agony. She couldn't be so stupid as to let it happen again.

But she had. Even as she tried to convince herself that she wasn't in love with Ben, she knew she was. He'd become the center of her life. It was too late to prevent it now; she could only hope that she was strong enough to withstand the pain and disappointment if they couldn't make it.

"Volunteers!" a woman called out. "We need some volunteers to umpire the kids' softball tournament. Volunteers. Come on, guys and gals. Equal-opportunity positions available."

Energy suddenly surged through Jessie's body. She needed to be busy, to keep her thoughts and fears from eating at her.

"I'll help," she said.

"Over there," the woman said, pointing. "Over at the north diamonds."

Jessie spun to smile at Ben. "You don't have to if you don't want to," she offered. "We can meet after the games."

Was she trying to get rid of him for a while? What good would being alone do, except to make her miss him?

Ben's frown told her he thought she was acting strangely, too. "I never pass up a chance to boss people around," he said, though his expression revealed the confusion he was experiencing.

Love? Why hadn't she seen it coming? But with each step she took, some of her fears seeped away until she reached over to take Ben's hand. His grasp was warm and strong, secure and safe.

Love! Maybe it wasn't the end of the world quite yet.

Jessie lay in Ben's arms, content and sleepy. She could hear his heart beating; the slow, steady rhythm echoed her own. Life had never been so sweet or good as today had been. He bent over to kiss her, a dreamy kiss that wasn't so much the end of the passion they'd just shared as it was a promise of passion for tomorrow and beyond. She couldn't believe how much she loved him.

"Did I tell you lately how beautiful you are?" Ben murmured.

"Not in the last five minutes." She snuggled closer against him and closed her eyes.

"I don't remember being able to talk much in the last five minutes. You have that effect on me."

"I haven't always," she said, thinking back to their first meeting.

"Always. I was just able to fight it better in the beginning."

She laughed and let sleep begin to wash over her. She'd had good times before, special times that had made her happy, but nothing like the contentment she felt here with Ben.

She knew she ought to be worried about the future, wondering how long they were going to last. But she just couldn't. She literally couldn't. She was basking in the sunshine of her love for Ben, and it wasn't in her power to bring clouds in to cover up the sun.

The sun. She and Ben were back at the picnic, and it was starting to storm. Everyone was running from the dark clouds that were covering up the sun, but she refused. She kept calling to the kids and other volunteers that it wasn't going to rain, but no one believed her. No one but Ben.

The wind started to blow, rattling the basketball net made of a lightweight chain, and some paper plates rolled across the softball field.

"It won't rain," she insisted. "It can't." But the storm sirens nearby began to ring.

"Jessie." Ben's voice was gruff and thick.

Was he doubting her love like the others?

"Jessie."

She felt Ben's hand on her arm and opened her eyes.

"Jess, your phone is ringing."

She sat up, staring disorientedly around her at the darkness. Her clock display showed that it was past four in the morning. The phone rang out a shrill beckoning at her bedside. The click of the answering machine silenced the noise just as consciousness fully arrived.

Jessie leaned on her elbows as she listened to her own voice advising the caller to leave their name, number and a short message after the beep. She rubbed her eyes as she glanced over at the window where Captain Kidd lay asleep on the sill, night breezes ruffling his fur just a bit. Even from where she lay, she could see the stars in the sky. There was no storm. Lord, she had been sound asleep.

The machine beeped and Tommy O'Rourke's voice came on. "Jessie. I'm down at the station with a young lady by the name of Maggie. That's all she'll give us. She was arrested for breaking and entering, and is asking for you. Give me a call when you can."

Jessie's sleepy, easy feeling fled as she sat up, reaching for her robe. "Maggie's never been in trouble before."

"You don't know that," Ben pointed out. "You don't know anything about the kid."

"You're right." Jessie got up and began to dress. "But she's never been in trouble here. We'd know if she had been."

Ben swung his feet to the floor. "She might be getting desperate, at the end of her rope. Or—" he stood up and reached for his pants "—she's just tired of being good."

"I'll call Tommy," Jessie said.

"I'll get the car," Ben suggested. "I can start looking into little Miss Mystery. See if I can find out where she's from and whether she has a record someplace else."

"Thanks." Jessie just flashed a smile at him as she reached under her bed for her sneakers, knowing she could depend on him. Together they would find out what there was to know about Maggie and would help her. That's what love was—someone to depend on.

The birds were just starting their early-morning chorus as Jessie and Ben crossed the apartment's parking lot to Ben's car. In another half-hour or so, the sun would be peeking over the horizon, sending its rays onto a yawning city shuffling into wakefulness.

Normally Jessie loved this time of the day. It was so fresh, prodigious with the promise of new adventures, new joys. But not today. Today was starting off with another poor kid in trouble.

"Want to go through the Doughnut House's drive-through for a quick breakfast?" Ben asked as he unlocked his car door for her.

Jessie shook her head as she slid into her seat. "I just want to get to the station as soon as we can."

"I'll get you something a little later, then," he said. "No telling how the day is going to go."

"Thanks."

She blinked back tears that started to form for some stupid reason. What was wrong with her that a simple sign of caring should turn on her emotional faucet? She must not be fully awake yet.

Ben revved the car engine and pulled out onto the street, moving along at a good pace. "You don't look too anxious to get down there," he noted.

Jessie just shook her head. "I am. It's just that I'm wondering what I can actually do for Maggie. Especially if she won't help me help her."

"You'll find a way. You have with lots of the kids at the center." He put his arm around her shoulder. Jessie gratefully accepted the refuge. "The kids just know instinctively you're someone who will always be in their corner when the bell rings."

Protected by his arm and soothed by his voice, Jessie closed her eyes and relaxed in the safe harbor that was Ben. His confidence in her gave her strength.

Maggie was going to be a challenge. Had been a challenge for a few weeks now, Jessie corrected herself. She'd been drawn to the girl since she'd first appeared at the center. Jessie had longed to reach out to her then, and was even more determined to now. This girl was special to her for some reason.

"I don't know what it is about Maggie," Jessie confided. "There's something about her...."

"It's those sunglasses she always wears," Ben teased. "Get her to take them off, and you'll find just a regular scared adolescent."

Jessie sighed as they pulled into the police station parking lot. "You're probably right."

"Of course I am," he replied. "Don't you remember? I'm always right."

"How silly of me to forget."

He pulled into his parking place and then pulled her into his arms. "You're going to do fine, lady. This kid's got all the luck in the world tonight to have you in her corner."

He kissed her then, as if to emphasize this point. It was a quick touch but, oh so sweet and lovely. So nice that she moved back closer for another, a much longer kiss that fortified her for the events ahead. Though she wished she could stay in his arms forever, she turned and pushed herself out of the car. They walked quickly into the building.

"Hi, Jessie. Ben." Tommy O'Rourke greeted them at the desk.

Ben nodded his greeting. "What do you have on the girl?"

"Nothing much," Tommy replied. "Simple B and E at the youth center. A window broken. No one hurt."

"Any priors?"

"Not here."

"Has she given you her full name?" Jessie asked.

Tommy shook his head. "Nope. But I checked our computer based on the MO and her physicals. She's a stranger to our system. No one at the youth center knows anything about her, either."

"She must be from out of town," Jessie said. The poor kid, feeling alone in the world.

"Maybe a runaway," Ben added.

Jessie nodded. That was where her thoughts had been heading. "Have you checked the runaway listings?"

"Don't think she's in them," Tommy said. "Some of the descriptions are pretty generic, but I called up some pictures through the computer and none seemed to match."

"Where are her parents, then?" Jessie said. "Haven't they noticed she's gone?"

"You know there's more to being a parent than just giving birth," Ben said, putting his arm around her shoulders. She knew he shared her pain, her outrage, and her love for him doubled and tripled.

"Whatever her background, I don't think she's a professional thief," Tommy said. "She didn't handle the B and E too smartly. And she's really spooked at being in here. She started asking for you, Jessie, as soon as she walked through the door. Showed us your card, like you were her lawyer."

Or maybe the only one who'd acted like she cared. What kind of parents did this girl have? "Where is she?" Jessie asked.

"Interrogation room C."

"I'll get her paperwork," Ben said.

Jessie nodded and started down the corridor. Some of the cases she had were often tragic; the kids had such terribly hard lives. But something had changed since Ben had come into her life. The cases still held the potential to rip her apart, but she had more strength with which to fight, more energy to battle the dragons of bureaucracy and an uncaring society. Maybe more of a belief that she could win.

Ben caught up with her and moved forward to open the door to room C. Jessie, shrouded in her invisible armor of professionalism, stepped briskly through the door. Following closely behind, Ben shut the door softly behind them.

Maggie was sitting on the other side of the table, staring at the scarred tabletop. She looked up as they stepped in.

The wraparound sunglasses were gone, showing the world what a scared little girl she was. Her face was dirtied, and tears had drawn streaks down her cheeks. Maggie's lips were quivering slightly.

Jessie saw this, and yet that wasn't what drew her attention. What she really saw were the bright, vividly blue eyes that looked up at her. Her own eyes were brown like her father's, but Denise and their brother, Danny, had those same blue eyes, just like their mother's.

Why did she think of that? Cold fingers of dread encircled Jessie's heart as she looked over and saw Ben watching her. Fears churned in her stomach as she felt his eyes reading the secrets of her soul.

Don't be silly, she scolded herself. It was just getting up so suddenly. She'd left her common sense somewhere back in the apartment. Without a word she reached for the girl's paperwork in Ben's hand and glanced quickly over it. Last name was left blank, as was address, birth date and age. Just the details of the breaking and entering at the youth center.

"What's your last name, Maggie?" Jessie asked.

"Evans."

The name meant nothing, rang no bells, and Jessie sat down, choosing the chair across from the girl. There were so many threads that she could follow, but which one would work the best? The only thing Jessie saw were those eyes. So blue and so like her mother's.

Her baby'd had blue eyes, but then all babies did. Jessie shouldn't let the memories flood her, prompted by something so commonplace as blue eyes. She had a job to do here.

"When's your birth date?"

It wasn't what Jessie meant to ask next, and even Ben seemed to know that, for he shifted in his chair next to her.

"My birthday?" Maggie stared for a minute, then shrugged. "June 3."

Jessie's heart stopped, frozen dead with anguish. It didn't mean anything, she told herself. No one had a lock on one certain day for their birthday. "And how old are you?" Jessie asked.

"Fourteen."

The world screeched to a halt, and Jessie had to force herself to breathe. So what? a voice inside her screamed. There had to have been lots of blue-eyed girls born that day. Blue-eyed baby girls were being born all the time, every day, everywhere. But Jessie couldn't seem to think; questions crowded her mind. Hope and fear warred with guilt, stealing her breath and sanity.

"Jessie."

Ben touched her hand and she looked up, reading the concern in his eyes. He knew something was wrong and wanted to help. But she had to look away; she couldn't let him see the fears and hope, the awful pain that must be reflected in her eyes.

Maggie couldn't be her child. She had a family all of her own that she'd run away from. It was just all a coincidence, but enough of one to bring back all the pain and doubts. It was something Jessie had to handle alone, had to bury once more deep within the dark corners of her heart.

"Ben." Her voice was audible, but just barely. "Can I see Maggie alone, please?"

His eyes asked for her trust, but she couldn't do it, and just turned toward Maggie, waiting Ben's murmured "Okay" and the soft closing of the door behind him.

Eight

Ben was worried. He knew he'd never seen Jessie begin an investigation, but once she got face-to-face with Maggie, she seemed so shaken. Her face had been pale, her voice almost trembling. How much longer could she last at this job, if each case tugged at her consciousness like this?

The computer he was sitting in front of finally spit out a message: the circuits were full. His data request would be processed in order received. The usual snafu. Ben went back to the interrogation room and knocked lightly on the door before opening it.

The kid was sitting where she had been, still staring down at the tabletop. Jessie was sitting next to her, listening. Neither of them looked up at him or seemed to notice when he sat down.

"I don't really remember Dad at all," Maggie was saying. "Though Mom had some pictures of him. After he died, we moved into this trailer the McGees had on their farm, and Mom would do their laundry and stuff.'' Maggie shrugged her shoulders. ''It was okay there, but then Mom got sick last winter. When she died, the McGees rented the trailer to somebody else even though I told them I could do the work Mom had been doing.''

Ben took advantage of the moment of silence to slide the computer's message over to Jessie. She glanced at it, then gave him a tight, little smile. She didn't look quite as tense as before, which relieved him, though her eyes seemed to burn.

He turned to Maggie. ''Don't you have any relatives? Family on your mother's or father's side?''

They waited a long moment before Maggie answered. ''Not really,'' she replied.

''Why weren't you referred to our social services department here?'' Jessie asked. ''Didn't anybody notify us when your mother died? We would have found you a foster home.''

Maggie fidgeted on the hard wooden chair. ''That was up in Michigan. We lived between White Pigeon and Constantine.''

Jessie started, her breath almost a cry. Ben tried to catch her eye, but she was writing something, or trying to. Her hand seemed to be trembling so much that he wondered how legible her writing would be. What had upset her so? The Michigan social services departments failed sometimes, just as the Indiana ones did.

Jessie seemed to have lost her composure, and he took up the slack. ''So how'd you end up in South Bend?'' he asked Maggie.

Maggie didn't answer. Probably ran away, Ben thought. Hitched a ride down here, not realizing that when you were homeless all cities were the same—cold and unfriendly. Except now that Jessie was on her side, South Bend wouldn't be that way.

Jessie seemed to have defeated whatever demons she'd been battling and leaned forward, closer to the girl. "When Ben asked you if you had family, you said, 'not really.' What did you mean by that?"

The girl scowled and stared hard at the tabletop.

"Maggie." Jessie's voice was so gentle, but with a core of steel.

"I was adopted," the girl mumbled. "Mom and Daddy weren't my real parents. So their relatives weren't really related to me."

Jessie sank back in her chair, almost as if she'd been struck. Her face was ashen, her eyes like those of a trapped fawn. Ben wanted to ask her what was wrong, wanted to hold her in his arms and protect her, but knew that she wouldn't want that now. He waited a moment for her to speak, and when she didn't, he turned to Maggie.

"Even if you're adopted into a family, the law still considers all of them your relatives," he pointed out.

"The law can't make them want you," Maggie snapped.

Jessie still didn't speak, not a word. Concern flooded his heart as Ben glanced at her, but Maggie needed an answer. There was a sullen curl to the kid's lip that Ben knew all too well.

"How do you know they didn't?" he asked her.

"They told me."

Jessie came alive again suddenly, reaching across the table to hold Maggie's hands in hers. "Oh, honey, I'm so sorry," she said. "You should have asked for help right away. I should have seen you needed help."

Ben really didn't like that. Jessie wasn't to blame for this girl's problems, and taking on that blame would only wear

Jessie down. She wouldn't have anything left to give anyone else. And it wasn't just himself that he was thinking of.

But then Jessie seemed to pull herself together more. She dragged her hands slowly away and sat up a little straighter.

"Have you or your family had any counseling to try to work out the problems?" she asked. "Have you talked to anybody about them? A social worker, a minister, teacher or someone at the youth center?"

The teenager shook her head.

"I knew they didn't want me, so I didn't hang around very long," Maggie replied.

"You ran away?" Ben asked.

Maggie shrugged. "I hung out other places. The youth center is a good place."

"That's fine for during the day," Jessie pointed out. She seemed to gather strength with each question. "Where did you stay at night?"

"I'd hide at closing time. When everyone was gone, I'd pull out the pads the little kids napped on. I slept good."

"What happened tonight?" Ben asked. "Why were you breaking into the center?"

"I had to go get some new shoes," Maggie replied, indicating the bright new sneakers on her feet. "I went to the department store on Western."

"You stole them," Ben said.

She shrugged as she had done so many times during the session. "I borrowed them, but I forgot that the buses don't run as often on Sunday. By the time I got back to the center, it was locked. And I didn't want to sleep outside because it's dangerous."

"You should have gone to the homeless shelter," Jessie said.

Maggie shook her head. "No way. They'd just call the cops. And the cops would take me back to the people I live with."

"Your family?" Ben asked.

Maggie didn't reply.

"Your sort-of family," he corrected.

She nodded.

It looked as if they were about to launch into another one of those long silences that they'd been playing with, and Jessie seemed to start fading again before his eyes.

"It's going to take us a while to straighten things out here," Ben said to Maggie. "How about if we all get some breakfast?"

For the first time that morning, the girl's face lit up. "Sure," she replied.

Ben stood up and reached for Jessie's hand. He hoped that breakfast would work for Jessie just as well as the idea of it perked up Maggie. Jessie was too important to him. He wasn't going to watch her fall apart like this and not do something.

Jessie followed Ben into his office. She felt drained, totally wiped out, and needed more than anything to be held in his arms. She knew she'd find strength there and peace, but also knew that she couldn't let herself lean on him. Not when that refuge might not be there for her much longer.

Jessie sank into a chair. Dear God. Could Maggie be the daughter she'd given away so long ago? Her eyes were stinging, and Jessie reached up to pinch the wetness away. She couldn't break down, not now.

"Kid's had some rough luck," Ben said as he sat down on the edge of Jessie's chair and kissed the top of her hair lightly.

"Yes."

He reached over to massage her shoulders as if reading her need. "Somebody should have been keeping an eye on her. A lot of people let her down, including her mother."

Jessie flinched. "How would her mother have known the trouble she was in? Once you give a child up for adoption, they don't tell you where she is."

Ben stopped his massage, though his hands stayed on her shoulders, lingering like in a last goodbye. "I meant her adopted mother," he said. "She should have made some arrangements for Maggie when she was sick. Hell, even before she got sick. She was the only one the kid had. She should have made provisions in case of some accident."

"I guess."

The pressure of his hands was too comforting. Jessie had to break away. She got to her feet and walked over to the window. The sun was up; the city was starting to come alive. Should she tell Ben of her suspicions now or wait until they knew more about Maggie?

"Well, I promised us all some breakfast and I'd better get hopping. Why don't you relax while I see what delicacies are in the vending machines?"

"Don't forget to get Maggie something."

Ben's look turned grim as he left the room, and Jessie closed her eyes, leaning against the window frame. Did he sense something? Did he sense that she had abandoned her child the same way his mother had abandoned him?

Oh, there were slight differences. Jessie had the excuse of the legal system barring her way, but that didn't exonerate her. She knew from her own professional experiences that adoptions didn't always work out. Just like in Maggie's case. She wasn't given to a bad set of adoptive parents; circumstances had just been against her. Jessie clenched her fists, trying to contain the anger that rose up in her stomach. She should have kept in touch. Made it her business to know where Maggie was and be ready in case things went bad. She had left her child's welfare to chance and deserved to pay the price.

"Coffee."

She blinked in consternation, trying to focus her mind and eyes. Ben was standing before her, holding out a disposable cup from which steam was wafting up.

"You okay?" he asked.

Jessie willed her hand to take the cup. "Just lost in thought. Thanks."

He was frowning, but nodded toward a napkin he'd put on his desk. Two glazed doughnuts were resting on it.

"Take your pick. Vanilla glazed or vanilla glazed."

"How can I choose?" She tried to joke, but it came out flat. She picked up one of the pastries and bit into it. Utter tastelessness. The coffee, too. She forced herself to eat anyway.

"I got the kid a bologna sandwich and a carton of milk to go with her snack. I figured she needed something a bit more substantial. She's had a rough night."

"True." Jessie went back to concentrating on the cup in her hands.

"Are you all right, babe?" he asked. "You look beat."

She shook her head. "Just thinking about Maggie and how alone she is."

"Well, her luck's changed," Ben said. "Now she's got you in her corner."

Oh, God. It was as if Ben had slapped her. Maggie should have always had her in her corner. Pain wrenched Jessie's heart, and she clenched her jaw for a long moment. "She seems like such a nice kid. How could those relatives not care about her?"

"We don't know that they don't," Ben pointed out. "We've only got her word to go on."

"No kid would stay away from home as much as she has if things weren't bad. Especially when she's hungry."

"Yeah, you're right," he agreed.

The coffee was losing what little appeal it had. Jessie put the cup on Ben's desk. The sting had returned to her eyes, and she blinked to keep them dry. Lately Ben was always there when she needed him, but she just didn't have the courage to put him to the test now.

Oh, how she wanted to tell him about Maggie! Tell him that she might very well be the daughter given away so long ago. Ask for his advice on how to approach the girl with that suggestion and what legal recourse would be available to her.

But she couldn't do any of that. Not with Ben, who still carried the hurt of his own mother's abandonment in his heart. People who can't take care of kids shouldn't have them. Those had been his very words. Once he learned the truth, he'd leave just as Randy had.

"I arranged to have Maggie taken over to Parkview," Ben said.

Jessie came awake with a thud. "The detention center?" She felt sick to her stomach. "Why? She's a first-time offender."

"We don't have anyplace else to put her at this hour," Ben pointed out. "We can't just release her back on the streets. She needs help, and most of the people who will provide that assistance aren't at work yet."

Jessie sighed. Ben was right; there was no place else to put Maggie. They had to wait until judges and other social welfare officials were available.

"Why don't I take you to my place?" he said, pulling her close. "Make you a real breakfast and put you to bed for a nice little nap?"

It felt too wonderful to be ensconced in his embrace, and his offer too tempting. She had to stop taking from him and gather some strength from within. "I should go home," she said, pushing herself away from him.

"Hey, nothing more than a little shut-eye," he said, raising his hand. "I promise."

She smiled at him, a slight smile but the best she could manage, and picked up her purse. "I wasn't worried that you had ulterior motives. I'd just rather go home."

He looked a long moment into her eyes, as if trying to read what lay behind her words, but she just stared at him resolutely. This was not the time to back down. She had to be alone, someplace where she could think. Think, and sort everything out.

Jessie opened the door and walked into her apartment, dragging her leaden feet along. Captain Kidd was on his usual wee-hours patrol, staring out the front window at the rays of sunshine sneaking up onto the city streets. Sparrows and blackbirds bickered among the evergreen bushes below, searching for breakfast crumbs.

She moved over to share the window seat with her cat. Normally he would have told her to go away, but this morning he said nothing after his initial one-eyed stare.

"What's wrong, Jess?" Ben had come up softly behind her, following in her wake after closing the door. "Honey?"

His voice was soft and caring. His embrace was strong yet gentle. She wanted so much to lean into him, to hide in the shelter of his arms, protected from the wintry winds of reality.

"You're so quiet," he said, "Are you okay?"

The obvious concern in his voice warmed her, yet Jessie knew she'd better get accustomed to its absence. "I'm just tired,'' she said. ''I guess I'm just not used to being jerked out of a sound sleep in the middle of the night.''

''Looks like you need more practice.''

He leaned down to kiss her gently on the forehead. The kiss, the words, the voice—they all combined to communicate a promise of warmth, a promise of love. A promise that Ben might not be able to keep.

''Maybe I'm getting a touch of burn-out,'' she said. ''There are so many kids, so much neglect, so little caring.''

He moved away from her, and she heard the chair by the window creak slightly as he lowered his weight into it, but she didn't trust herself to look at him. Seeing him here, his presence making her apartment seem a home, would only make the emptiness later more painful.

''We've both seen kids in worse trouble,'' Ben said.

Jessie leaned against the wall, disturbing the drapes behind her but not caring. She reached over to scratch behind Captain Kidd's ears, watching the trails her fingers left in her cat's fur. Just to be in Ben's arms for one more minute would be heaven.

''She was checked out by the emergency docs at Memorial,'' Ben went on. ''She's never been physically abused and she doesn't seem to be emotionally troubled.''

The cat squeaked a note of protest, so Jessie stopped scratching, folding both arms across her chest. She watched Captain Kidd's tail flick back and forth, hitting her knee.

''I'm not saying she's totally problem free,'' Ben said. ''But that's understandable. She's lost both her parents and doesn't appear to have any other family. Her depression is to be expected.''

Jessie turned toward the window. More and more sunshine was climbing up over the horizon. Holding fast and warming the inhabitants until the soldiers of night took over.

Back and forth they went, every day. Which would eventually be the victor: the sunshiny bright joy of day or the darkness of night?

Ben had seen a lot in his years on the force. Would he understand her actions, or would the pain from his own childhood override everything else? Was Randy's desertion just his irresponsibility or what she should expect from any man?

"She looks like a tough kid," Ben said. "I'm sure once things settle down she'll land on her feet."

Land on her feet. Jessie's hand dropped down to Captain Kidd's ears again. That made Maggie sound like a cat, a stray that had to shift for itself. Captain Kidd jumped down off the windowsill and, muttering and grumbling under his breath, made his way to the bedroom.

Jessie knew she had to do something. She couldn't continue to avoid Ben's eyes forever, but neither did she have the strength to look at him and then look away. His blue eyes would invite her into their depths, would offer her a soothing place to relax and find peace. But sooner or later she'd have to tell Ben the truth about her past. She stared outside once more, the street scene blurring, losing its sharp edges and taking on an impressionistic quality.

What would she tell him? That fourteen years ago last month she had given up her daughter. That she'd been a child herself and unable to care for another child. That she had given the girl up so she could have a better life than any Jessie could give her.

Would he understand how she had tossed and turned, wrestling with the decision? Or would he see only the similarities to what his mother had done?

"You should get some sleep," Ben said. "Maybe take the morning off."

Take the morning off! If Maggie was her child, Jessie had already taken fourteen years off of her responsibility to the child. "I just need a shower," Jessie said.

Maggie needed her. That was the simple truth. No matter how much she loved Ben, Jessie had Maggie's welfare to consider. The cost to herself wasn't important.

The chair made some soft noises as it gave up Ben's weight. She could feel him moving toward her.

"Sometimes," he said, "there is no reasonable explanation for why a case really grabs us."

A case? No, Maggie could be her daughter.

"When we hit a situation like that," Ben went on, "it's best to walk away. Get another professional to take over, someone who's still objective."

What was he saying? Turn her back on another child? But she couldn't, not even if it would mean jeopardizing her relationship with Ben.

"If we're not objective," he told her, "a lot of people can get hurt. Including ourselves and those we are trying to help."

Jessie was already hurting, hurting with the knowledge of how she might have failed Maggie and how she would hurt Ben. But there was nothing she could do about that. There was no way out without someone paying the cost, and it couldn't be Maggie anymore.

Would Ben be a part of that future? She didn't know, but it would be his choice. She would find the right time to tell him and let him choose. Now was not the time, though. She had to be stronger first; she had to learn to live on her own once more.

"Well," she said, turning from the window with a smile, "I think I'll take that shower now. I've got to work."

Without a word Ben came closer and took her into his arms. She felt the tenderness of his embrace, knowing it could be for the last time. She loved him desperately, but she loved her daughter, too. There were no choices to be made.

It might be true that it was better to have loved and lost than to have never loved at all. But not by much.

Jessie was back at work by ten o'clock, and immersed in Maggie's case by 10:01. The busier she kept, taking care of Maggie, the less time she'd have to think about Ben. She began trying to track down Maggie's files in Michigan.

"It's imperative that I have the girl's files immediately," Jessie said sharply into the phone. "Ship it by the fastest way possible. I'll pay whatever it costs."

A long pause of silence told Jessie her counterpart in Michigan's St. Joseph County was pondering her course of action. The other woman was young, probably a recent college graduate, and wasn't sure what the proper procedures were.

"I guess I could send it by express mail," the woman said, uncertainty hanging on the wires.

"That'll take three days," Jessie snapped. "I need that file by this afternoon."

"There's no way to do that."

Jessie's mouth was opened, ready to pour angry words in the woman's ear. But the young woman in Michigan was right. There was no sensible way to do that, and it wasn't as if Jessie absolutely had to have the file. Her reasons were purely selfish; curiosity had gotten the best of her. Maggie would be in Parkview for the next few days because of the slowness of her own legal system, nothing else.

"Could you look in the file and verify a piece of information?" Jessie asked. "Could you find out if the girl was adopted?"

Some page rustling mixed with the background of silence, so Jessie knew the woman was looking. She waited, biting her lip, while a torrent of emotions raced through her. What if this was all a wild-goose chase? What if Maggie had made up the whole story to gain sympathy and the rollercoaster ride of hopes and fears Jessie was on was unnecessary? Jessie didn't know what to hope for. She didn't want to lose Ben, but neither did she want to lose the chance of finding her daughter.

"Yes."

The woman's answer hung in the air until Jessie found the ability to speak again. "I don't suppose the biological mother is listed?"

"No. That kind of information has been sealed by the courts."

"Of course," Jessie said. "Just send that file via express delivery and have your supervisor call me if there are any problems."

The young woman agreed, and Jessie slowly hung up the phone. Excitement as well as depression came to sit on her shoulders. She wanted Maggie to be her daughter, but she was so afraid of Ben's rejection. Would she always be this torn apart?

Her phone rang, and Jessie grabbed it up to stem her thoughts.

"Hi, lover."

Yesterday that single word would have set her heart to dancing, but today she tasted a bittersweet combination. Joy tempered by sadness and fear.

"Hi," she answered, trying to keep her voice light.

"How are you?" he asked.

"Fine, fine." Jessie knew that her voice wasn't quite hacking it, so she rushed in to fill Ben's concerned silence. "Have you gotten the address for Maggie's relatives?"

"Yes."

The tone was slow, reluctant. He hadn't really wanted to tell her.

"What is it?" Jessie asked, picking up a pencil.

He waited and Jessie could feel her stomach tensing up. She knew that he was thinking of telling her to drop the whole thing. Get someone else to go, someone objective. But he didn't know why this girl's case was so important to her.

"Why don't I come by and pick you up?" he said. "I'll take you out there."

Her mouth opened and then shut. She didn't want an argument, but she didn't want any more pain, either. "Okay."

The ride to Maggie's relatives overflowed with silence. Jessie tried to release the memories of the laughter they'd shared in the car on other drives, or the emotions that had smoldered there, waiting for a chance to be shown. Having this man in her life was like icing on a cake—sweet and wonderful, but not a necessity.

Ben stopped in front of a small house on the city's west side. All the houses on the block were worn, but this one appeared shabbier than the rest. An old woman answered their knock, gray strands of hair escaping her bun, a drab dress covering her bony shoulders and sharp eyes checking them both out.

"Police, ma'am," Ben said, showing his badge. "And this is Miss Taylor from the county's social service unit. Could we come in, please?"

The woman hesitated, then, with a noticeable sigh unlocked the screen door to let them in. The same tiredness that clothed the exterior greeted them as they stepped into the living room. An old man sat in a wheelchair in front of a small TV set.

"We have Maggie at Parkview," Ben said. "The juvenile house of detention."

The woman sighed, her face sagging even more. "Wondered where she'd gone to," the woman murmured.

"You haven't called the police," Jessie accused.

"That girl's gonna do what she's gonna do," the old woman answered. "Don't matter none what I do."

Jessie had come here expecting to be angry, in fact looking forward to it. But the sight of the shabby house tempered that anger. And now, here in the presence of the woman's defeat, that hostility evaporated.

What good would anger do? The woman was obviously strained to the edge of her resources, financial, physical, emotional, whatever. Lashing out at the woman would be like beating a dead horse.

"What's your relation to Maggie?" Jessie asked.

The woman shrugged. "I'm a second or third cousin of her momma, the one who adopted the child."

"Was that in Michigan?"

"Yeah." The woman nodded. "Up in St. Joseph County. I think the child were born in White Pigeon."

Cold fingers seized her heart, but Jessie was used to them. She just clutched her purse for a moment as if it could steady her, wishing instead she could clutch at Ben's hand.

"Do you have any objections to Maggie being placed in a foster home?" Jessie asked.

Defeat rode the woman's shoulders like a jockey on a racehorse. "Whatever the child wants is okay by me."

Jessie nodded, looking around. There would be no problem authorizing Maggie to be removed from this atmosphere. They made their farewells and eased themselves out of the house.

Ben started back toward downtown, and Jessie just stared out the window. Maggie was her child. She was sure of it now, and it was time to reclaim her, but she had to go about it professionally.

First she'd start the paperwork to get herself licensed as a foster parent, so when Maggie got out of the detention center, she could come home to Jessie. After that was all done, Jessie would start adoption proceedings so Maggie would be hers legally.

"I'm going to file a request to become a licensed foster mother," she said, her words seeming loud in the silence that had surrounded them lately.

Ben turned to her, frowning in disbelief, concern making his eyes seem dark and stormy. "Jess, haven't you got enough heartbreak working with these kids each day? When are you going to relax if you're going home to more kids?"

"Not kids. Kid. Just one."

He sighed. Weariness or impatience? "Maggie."

"She needs me," Jessie said.

The words hung in the air, waiting for challenge or retraction, but neither came. This was the time to tell him, to confess her past, but she couldn't. Not driving down Western Avenue, where he had to concentrate on the traffic.

"I just feel it's something I have to do," she said quietly.

"How can you help them if you get emotionally involved with each one?"

"Why would I want to help them if I wasn't?"

Ben's hands tightened around the steering wheel, his knuckles white with the strain, but it was a moment before he spoke to her. "I'm just afraid you're taking on too much," he finally said.

"I know what I'm doing," she said. Why then did she feel as though she were wandering blindly in the dark so much of the time?

"You going to softball practice tonight?"

"No."

He said nothing more, but turned at Main Street. Everything about him said he was upset, everything but his words. His jaw was tight, his shoulders rigid, and his glance never left the road to sweep gently over her. He stayed silent. It was as if the silence were building a wall between them.

Jessie knew it was her fault, knew what words she'd have to say to make the wall disappear, but who could guarantee that her confession would penetrate the barrier?

He pulled up in front of her office, and she hopped out of the car. "Thanks," she mumbled, shutting the door and racing up the steps before he could stop her.

He didn't seem to have tried.

Nine

Jessie grabbed at her folders and hurried into the conference room before she dropped them. She made it, but dropped them anyway upon seeing Ben standing there.

"Hi," she mumbled, then retreated to the safety of picking up her papers. No safety there, though, for he came over to help her.

His woodsy after-shave wafted around her, reminding her of hungers and love fulfilled, of nights of love and days of joy. His hand brushed hers, starting her heart pounding, but she forced strength into her smile and grabbed up the rest of the papers. It had only been two days since she'd seen him, two days that had lasted an eternity, and she wasn't going to fall apart.

"How have you been?" he asked.

"Busy." She laid her papers on the conference table. "I didn't know you'd be here."

"Somebody from the department had to come. Maggie was arrested, after all."

"I just thought..." She shrugged her words away. Of course he would have come. Why hadn't she prepared herself for the probability of seeing him? Because she had refused to think about him at all, that's why.

"Jess, what's going on?" He took her hand before she could find a way to look busy. "Have I done something?"

"Of course not. I told you, I've just been busy. Maggie's never been in the system before, and there's been a lot of paperwork."

"So you're going through with this." His eyes tried to pull her into their depths.

She pulled both her hands and her eyes away. "Maggie needs a home."

Ben looked ready to open the whole discussion again, but a knock at the door stopped him. The director of the youth center, came in.

"Hi, Harry." Jessie's greeting was a bit more enthusiastic than necessary, but she was so glad to see him. She didn't need more time alone with Ben. Not until she had everything sorted out in her mind.

"Why don't we all sit down?" Jessie suggested, taking the chair at the head of the table. "Harry, since Maggie's crime involved the youth center, I wanted you here to hear where we're at with the case. We're—" She stopped and glanced quickly at Ben. His eyes told her nothing. "I'm hoping that you'll agree to drop the charges once you hear the whole story."

She half expected Ben to argue, but he just watched her. That was almost worse than his arguing. She took a deep breath and outlined Maggie's background for Harry, starting with her adoption and her father's death, going through her mother's death and the condition of her relatives' home life.

"Plus this is her first offense," Jessie concluded.

"She admitted to stealing the shoes," Ben pointed out.

"Because she had no support to get the things she needed," Jessie said. "Once she's in a foster home with someone to take care of her, she won't steal again."

Ben looked skeptical, but it was Harry who spoke. "Can you be sure of that, though? I hate to be critical, but we all know that not all foster homes give the kids the support they need."

"Maggie's will," Jessie said. "She's going to be living with me."

"Really?" Harry was more than pleased; he was excited for her. "That's great. God, you give a lot to these kids."

Ben said nothing, not that Jessie was going to give him a chance to. "What I'd like to do, Harry, is have Maggie perform some community service work. I know it won't pay for the broken window, but I'd hoped you could find some chores for her around the center. Have her take some responsibility for her actions."

"Sounds great to me. We can always use some extra hands."

Jessie looked over at Ben, only meeting his eyes for the barest of seconds.

"My department has no trouble with that."

"Great. I'll get the paperwork settled." Jessie was amazed that the meeting had gone so quickly. She had feared a reprisal from Ben.

"Well, I gotta run." Harry was already at the door. "Big meeting with the mayor looking for ways to get funding."

Jessie barely had time to wish him good luck before he was gone. She gathered up her folders and found Ben leaning against the closed door. No sneaking out.

"You going to Parkview now?" he asked.

"That's what I planned."

"I'll drive you."

Her arguments that it wasn't necessary fell on deaf ears, and a few minutes later she was seated in Ben's car. For a wonderful moment she let herself relax, let herself feel the goodness and rightness of being here with him. Then the memories of so many precious moments came flowing around her, and she had to push them away.

"I don't have anything against Maggie," Ben said suddenly. "She seems like a nice kid. I'm just worried about you."

"I know, but you don't have to."

He glanced her way, his eye not so disapproving as confused, pained. Jessie bit her lip and stared down at her hands in her lap. She wasn't being fair to him.

The rest of the ride was silent, strained and painful. Jessie tried to focus on Maggie and what she would say to the girl, but her eyes kept drifting over to Ben. The movement of his hands on the steering wheel brought back memories of his hands on her, the pleasures, the laughter that his touch could awaken.

She was glad once they got to Parkview and Maggie joined them. "So, how are things going?" Jessie asked the girl.

"Okay."

The tone was tough and belligerent, but Maggie's eyes were wide with a barely concealed fear.

"We went to visit your cousin," Jessie said. "The one you were staying with in South Bend. She has a hard row to hoe."

The girl's shoulders slumped. "She was always crabbing at me. I try to be good, but then she starts crabbing at me and I get mad all over."

"We're arranging for you to go to a foster home once you're released from here. Do you have any other relatives or close friends you'd like to stay with?"

Maggie just shook her head. Her eyes kept going over toward Ben, though he hadn't said a word so far.

"You aren't going to jail or reform school or anything like that," he told her, and Maggie's shoulders sank in visible relief. "Miss Taylor convinced the youth center to let you do work there, and they won't press charges."

Maggie's face tried to hide her emotion behind a cool facade, but she didn't quite make it. "Thank you so much," she said to Jessie. "I won't ever do anything like that again. I promise."

"I know you won't," Jessie said. She tried to smile her thanks at Ben, grateful and touched that he had seen a worry in Maggie that she hadn't. And that he had responded to that need. But he didn't meet her glance.

"I'm more concerned about the shoes you stole," he said, effectively putting a pall over the child's joy and Jessie's gratitude. From a rush of love for him, she went to a flash of anger.

Maggie's glow also faded. "I used to do some baby-sitting when Mom was still alive. Maybe once I get a home here, I can baby-sit some more and pay for the shoes."

"I think that's a wonderful idea," Jessie said. She reached across the table and squeezed Maggie's hand. "There's a couple of women in my building who are always looking for baby-sitters. You're going to be kept busy."

Maggie just stared at her, and Jessie realized that her words must not have made much sense to the girl.

"I'm applying for a foster parent license," Jessie told her. "And once I get it, you can live with me."

Maggie blinked once and then quickly lowered her eyes. Had there been a spark in the girl's eyes? Jessie was sure there was. But was it a spark of anger or one of eager anticipation? She looked at Ben for reassurance, an automatic reaction that she cursed herself for. She turned her eyes back to Maggie, not allowing herself time to read anything in Ben's eyes.

"I have an apartment," Jessie said. "But it's a nice place. And I have a cat named Captain Kidd. I named him after an old pirate. He's only got one good eye and he's always swaggering around like he owns the place."

"I always wanted a pet. Will he let me comb him?"

"As long as you admit he's boss," Ben said.

Maggie seemed surprised at his answering, and looked from him back to Jessie. This was hardly the point in this whole mess for Maggie to make any assumptions, so Jessie jumped into speech.

"It's going to take me a couple more days to work everything out. I know it seems long, but the court and everyone has to check a bunch of things out."

"No problem," Maggie replied. "I can take anything for a few days. Mom always said I was tough."

Jessie's throat tightened up. Her daughter was tough, that was for sure. She'd had to be. And now was the time for Jessie to be tough. To do whatever she had to for her daughter.

"I'll keep in touch," Jessie said, her voice almost a whisper.

"I ain't going nowhere," Maggie said, an impish grin creeping onto her lips.

Jessie stood and Ben followed. "See you soon."

They walked out to the car in silence. Jessie could feel Ben getting ready to voice his worries again, but she wouldn't listen.

"My office is the other way," Jessie said.

Ben glanced at her, trying to hide his worry behind a smile. "Yeah, I know, but some friends had been asking about you, and I promised to bring you for a visit."

"What friends?"

Ben drove around the back of Memorial Hospital. The sun shining off the river winked at them from the end of the street. He parked the car next to the duck pond.

Jessie didn't smile, though, and her eyes looked sad. "I don't have anything for them."

"I brought something." He pulled a bag of stale bread from behind the front seat.

"Were you a Boy Scout?" Jessie asked.

"You mean like in always prepared?" Ben shook his head and opened the door to get out. "Nope. That's an organization for middle-class kids. It was a little out of my reach."

He took her hand, and they walked down to the ducks' enclosure. A number rushed over, demanding treats.

"I sure wouldn't risk arming these waddling little buggers," he said, and was rewarded with a slight smile. It didn't last very long or go very deep, so he went on. "They're asking about you. Want to know where the heck you've been."

Leaning her arms on the fence, Jessie watched the birds. "I've been busy, guys."

The ducks and geese continued their quacking and squawking.

"I think they're saying cut the gab and pass the grub."

Laughing, she took the bread and broke off pieces to throw to the birds. After emptying the bag, she just stood there, staring at the ducks pushing and squabbling. Her face was more relaxed, as if she'd thrown off some of her cares and dumped them in the river. Ben felt some of his own tensions evaporate.

He'd always thought Jessie to be the ultimate professional. She was dedicated and caring, giving her all for the people she served. Yet she didn't let their situations suck her dry as a person. She always seemed able to protect her soul, so no matter how exhausted she was, there was always enough of herself left to regenerate for another day. Or at least that was how he used to see her.

Now she seemed to have lost that wall of protection. Somehow this thing with Maggie had wormed its way into her heart. If she wasn't careful, it would yank her heart by the roots and kill her powers of recuperation.

Jessie was really obsessed with this kid. But why this particular kid? What was there about this latest street waif that enabled her to break into the inner recesses of Jessie's soul?

"I should be going," Jessie said quietly. "I have a lot to do."

She didn't make a move toward his car, so Ben kept leaning on the fence.

They'd spent a lot of time together, yet Ben was realizing that he really didn't know Jessie. She'd given him a little background on herself, but he'd avoided asking the questions that would pull them closer, that would have given him a glimpse into her soul. Why? A leftover from his married years, when that knowledge and closeness had been a burden? Now, though, when he needed to know Jessie in order to help her, he felt lost and helpless.

Jessie looked at her watch. "I really have to get back to my office," she said. "I've got a million things waiting for me."

Small, tiny ripples darted across her cheeks. Were they the result of anger or exhaustion? Ben didn't really know what to make of Jessie's emotions, except that they were strong. Grounded in some deep-rooted feelings that he couldn't identify, much less understand. The only thing he knew for sure was that it was best not to push. The only thing he could do with this storm was to ride it out.

"I'm making dinner tonight," he said.

Jessie barely nodded.

"Spaghetti and fried chicken," Ben said. "And you're going to be there."

He held his breath a moment as he watched her face. Suddenly the tension dissolved into a weak sort of smile, but a real smile nonetheless.

"It's nice to know what I'll be doing this evening," she said. "It's such a bother trying to manage an active social calendar like mine."

Ben's throat was tight and he leaned forward, kissing Jessie gently on her lips. The tightness descended, plunging on down to basic. He took her in his arms, the better to kiss her. He did and she did. It was the kind of partnership he'd thought they had, but the kiss was over way too soon as Jessie pulled away. His heart was chilled.

This was it, Jessie thought as she walked up the steps to Ben's house. All afternoon she'd thought about canceling their dinner date, but knew that running from the situation wasn't going to solve anything. She had to tell Ben the truth about Maggie. It was going to be hard, but it was time. She owed him that honesty.

"Hi, Jess." Ben had the door open and was waiting for her.

"Hi."

She stepped inside, feeling the peace and security of his home surround her. It was a dangerous pull, this urging to leave all her worries outside the door and forget about everything but now. She fought it, though, cloaking herself in determination and holding the thought of Maggie close to her heart.

Ben closed the door behind her and then took her into his arms. "God, I've missed you," he murmured. He didn't kiss her, just held her as if he were afraid she might run away.

She didn't exactly, but neither did she linger. There was no bravery in flirting with danger; wisdom lay in avoiding it, and she planned to be very wise tonight. She gently pulled herself away from Ben, feeling his loss with a bitter pang.

If he noticed her retreat, he didn't show it. "Want a glass of wine?"

"Sure." It would give her something to hold, an excuse to be out of his arms.

"Have a seat," Ben said. "I'll be right back."

Jessie chose a chair rather than the sofa and silently rehearsed her speech, but doubts washed over her. Should she break the relationship off, then tell him about Maggie? Should she tell him about her daughter, then wait for him to break it off? What if he didn't want to end it? What if he wanted to, but didn't know how to say it?

"Here you go, babe."

He gave her a glass of a blush wine, then sat down across from her on the sofa. She wanted to join him there, to sit next to him and let him hold her while she poured out her soul, but knew that would never work. She'd never tell him the truth if her heart felt the joy of his touch again; she wouldn't have the strength.

"Everything's ready if you'd like to eat," Ben said after a long moment.

"Sure. Need any help?" she asked.

"Nope, I have everything under control." They went into the kitchen. "Although a sweet smile to spur me on would help."

Jessie tried, but was glad that he didn't watch her for too long. A smile she could manage, but not for any duration. He busied himself serving the dinner, though, and Jessie felt herself relax a tad.

"You went to a lot of work," Jessie said.

Ben shook his head as he put a basket of Italian bread on the table. "Not really. Only the salad needed work. Opening a bottle of wine and defrosting some spaghetti sauce ranks as minimal labor." He put the platter of spaghetti in the middle of the table and sat down. "Well, dig in."

Jessie tried to eat, but her thoughts were on the upcoming discussion and her heart was too afraid. She played with her food, pushing it from one side to another, hoping Ben wouldn't notice.

"How about some salad?" Ben asked.

She noticed he hadn't eaten much, either. "I think I must be getting one of those summer colds," she said, and took some salad.

"That's about enough to starve a baby rabbit," Ben said.

Jessie chose not to respond to his remark. She poured salad dressing onto the lettuce. Maybe it was a mistake to wait for the right moment to begin. Maybe there was no right time.

"I thought Maggie was holding up real well," she said.

"No reason she shouldn't," Ben said. "That's not the black hole of Calcutta she's in."

His voice wasn't exactly unfeeling, but there was a tone to it she didn't like, an anger that lay under the words.

"Well, excuse me," Jessie snapped. "I'd forgotten what a Mr. Sensitive you were."

Ben's cheeks reddened. "I know there are better places," he said. "But there are also a whole lot worse places she could be in."

"She 'could' be in?" Jessie asked. "Or do you mean 'should' be in?"

He put his fork down and pushed the salad away. "Let's not analyze every damn word that comes out of my mouth. Better yet, let's just forget about it."

She went back to shoving the lettuce and tomato around her plate, fighting back tears that were suddenly threatening. She didn't want to fight with him, didn't know how not to, either.

"Jess, honey," he implored. "This has been a hell of a week, and I just wanted the two of us to relax. Put all the serious stuff behind us and—"

"You mean Maggie. You want me to put Maggie behind us and forget all about her." There was a wrenching pain in her heart, an agony that begged him to deny her words. She pushed her plate away, through with the facade of eating.

"For tonight, yes," Ben said. "You need a little time off. Time to relax."

"And that's your specialty, isn't it? Fun and games." Things became clearer. More painful, too, as Jessie's fears were realized.

She got to her feet, fighting back her tears and letting anger take hold. "That was one of the first things you told me. Fun and games. Nothing serious between us."

Ben got to his feet also, shaking his head. "What are you talking about?"

"Well, life isn't just fun and games," she said, spitting the words out. "There is pain and there is need. And Maggie needs a lot more than fun and games right now."

"Jess, I—"

But Jessie was in no mood for reconciliation. Maggie needed her, more than Ben ever would; that was all too clear now. "So, since I can't fulfill your needs, like fun and games, I guess I'm out."

"What the hell are you talking about?"

She stood behind her chair, leaning her hands on the back of it for support. "I'm talking about the fact that someone else needs me and you can't handle that."

"What I can't handle is how you've let this one kid become an obsession with you."

"Obsession?" Jessie felt as if he'd hit her, knocking all the wind from her sails. The chair was no longer any support. She stepped back, wrapping her arms across her chest. "That obsession, as you so quaintly put it, is my daughter."

"What you need, Jess, is a little time to—" The words must have suddenly sunk in, for he stopped. "Your what?"

Jessie felt ready to crumble, but wouldn't allow herself that luxury. She didn't have strength for more arguing, though. "I'm not absolutely sure," she said quietly. "But I think Maggie is the daughter I gave up fourteen years ago, when I was sixteen. It was soon after my mother died and I was... I was rather vulnerable."

"You had a child?"

"Yes, damn it. Yes."

Jessie turned away from him for a long moment, watching the evening shadows creep across his backyard. The day was over, and soon it would be night. She fought back the pain, the tears, the guilt. There'd be time for all that later. When she turned back to him, she was under control.

"No one in my family, most of all me, was in any emotional shape to care for a baby. Adoption looked like the best for all concerned, especially the child."

He sank into his chair like a weary prizefighter in the ring, taking one blow after the other. But he said nothing. His eyes reflected his surprise, but deep below that, she could see anger. Was he judging her and finding her the same as his mother?

"You're sure a bagful of surprises," he said. "We weren't very close, were we?"

Sure, throw the blame on her. ‘‘We were just what you wanted,’’ Jessie snapped, knowing, though, that she had broken their rules. ‘‘Good-time buddies.’’

‘‘What we wanted,’’ he corrected his voice bitter.

‘‘Right.’’ It seemed so long ago, that evening they had talked about love and disappointment and friendship. She’d been so incredibly stupid, it was hard to believe that it was only two weeks ago. It seemed a lifetime. ‘‘It was what we both wanted, just somebody to have some fun with.’’

‘‘And now you’ve got somebody else, and this is your gentle way of letting me know.’’

‘‘It’s not like that,’’ she argued. ‘‘You make it sound like I found someone else to go to the movies with, so I don’t want to go with you.’’

He got up again and began to clear the table. His movements were slow, and his eyes were dull. ‘‘No, it’s what I should have expected,’’ he said. ‘‘You admitted to devoting your life to your work. I should have realized when a case came along that you could really sink your teeth into, that I’d easily be replaced. With Maggie around, you can be a bleeding heart for twenty-fours a day, instead of just twelve with me.’’

‘‘My God, you make me sound sick,’’ Jessie cried. ‘‘Maggie’s my daughter, she’s not just some case.’’

‘‘How do you know she’s your daughter?’’ he asked. His eyes, when he glanced up at her, were tinged with anger again. ‘‘Adoption records are sealed in every state.’’

Jessie took a deep breath, trying to stem the pain that stabbed at her when he looked her way. ‘‘Her birth date is right. She was adopted near White Pigeon and she has my mother’s eyes.’’

‘‘And on that flimsy evidence, you’re devoting your whole life to that kid.’’

That kid! ‘‘Why do you hate her so?’’ Jessie cried.

Ben just looked at her. "I don't hate her," he said. His voice was quiet, and she knew he was telling her the truth. "I just hate what she's doing to you. No, that's unfair. I hate what you're doing to yourself."

"It's what I have to do."

He shrugged and went back to clearing the table. "It's funny in a way. First I got tossed aside by a woman wanting life, not her kid. Now you're tossing aside your life, wanting your kid."

She waited for a moment, a long silent eternity, wanting him to say that he could accept Maggie into his life, too. But he didn't. He didn't say anything. Jessie guessed that she needn't have worried about what route to take in telling him. It went just as she'd expected, just as it had with Randy.

"I guess I should be going," Jessie said.

Ben didn't reply.

"Want me to help clean up?"

He shook his head.

Jessie's feet seemed mired in quicksand, unable to move, but finally she got them going and headed toward the door. He didn't stop her; he didn't say a word.

"Goodbye, Ben."

It was more a whisper, a prayer for understanding, but his back was to her and he didn't turn. Jessie let herself out the door, tears streaming down her face. It was over and love had been true to form. Tore her apart and left her bleeding.

Ben heard Jessie's goodbye, but he couldn't speak. He didn't dare. One little word, and the tears and all the hurt would come pouring out. It was over. So what difference would all of that make? It would just give Jessie more pain. He heard the door close quietly and he sat down, staring out at the darkening shadows on the lawn.

Sometime later—a few minutes or a few hours later, he didn't know which—he stood up. He turned on the lights and blew out the candles, then finished cleaning up.

The last thing on the table was the bottle of wine. He stared at it for a long moment and then slowly poured it down the drain.

Ten

Jessie gave the attendant her papers and waited for Maggie, jiggling from one foot to the other. Maggie was finally coming home. Fourteen years late, but she'd finally be where she belonged. The only thing that would have made Jessie happier was if Ben had been here and the two of them were taking Maggie home together.

The door to the girls' area opened, and Jessie shut out all thoughts of Ben. She had hardly slept the past two nights and jumped every time the phone rang at work. But Ben was gone—out of her life, never to return. Jessie concentrated her attention on the child standing stiffly just inside the room.

"Hi," Jessie said.

"Hi," Maggie replied.

They stood there and stared at each other. What did she do now? Take the girl by the hand and lead her out? Maggie was fourteen, a little too old to be led. Should she just tell her to come? Maggie wasn't her prisoner. Or should she just walk out and let the girl follow her? That wouldn't be very friendly.

"She's free to go," the attendant said.

"Oh, fine," Jessie said quickly at the same time that Maggie moved toward her. The attendant had solved the problem for both of them.

They walked out of the detention center side by side. "My car is the red one at the far end," Jessie said, reaching in her pocket as they stepped out into the parking lot. Her fingers searched frantically through her coat pocket. "Oh, no. I couldn't have."

Maggie was peering in the window on the driver's side. "You locked your keys in," she said.

Swallowing hard, Jessie reminded herself to stay calm. "Wait here," she said. "I'll run in and get a coat hanger."

"I'll take care of it," Maggie said, rushing back to the center. Within seconds she was back with a "hot shot" in her hands, a long, narrow, thin piece of metal Jessie knew car thieves used. Maggie slipped it in between the window and the door frame, popping up the door lock in less than a half second.

"You mess up your paint job with a coat hanger," Maggie said, pointing out the scratches Jessie had already inflicted. "This tool is quicker and doesn't hurt the finish. Your cop boyfriend should have told you that."

"Where'd you get that?" Jessie asked, not daring to ask her how she knew how to use it.

"From the office. They took it off one of the kids yesterday when he got brought in."

"Oh." Jessie got into the car and unlocked the passenger door for Maggie.

"Where is he anyway?" Maggie asked as she slammed the door closed.

"Where is who?"

"Your cop boyfriend." Maggie rolled her eyes heavenward. "The one that's always tagging after you."

Jessie turned her eyes to the front, checking out the quiet street scene before them. Her hand shook slightly, but she got the ignition turned. She took a deep breath and waited a moment.

"He's really busy," Jessie said, and put the car in gear. "We won't be seeing that much of him."

She told herself it didn't matter, that her life was full now. But even in the joy of bringing Maggie home, Jessie knew that was a lie.

"How is your new family coming along?"

Jessie looked up from the books she was gathering together after her class and smiled at the middle-aged woman who asked.

"Real good," Jessie told her student. "Maggie helps with the housework and during the day she helps out at the West Side Youth Center. I don't have to worry about her at all."

"Sounds great," the woman said.

"Yep," Jessie said. "Everything is just perfect."

The woman bade her a good-night, but once she was gone and Jessie was alone, she let her face fall. It was true what she had said about Maggie. The girl was great, but things were far from perfect.

Jessie's life had always been full, what with her work, her volunteer activities, her sports teams and now Maggie. One would think that Ben could easily have been squeezed out.

But that wasn't the way things were working out. It was as if that damn man had created his very own space in her life—in her heart. So no matter how much she crammed in, that awful empty ache remained.

She viciously stuffed books and papers into her overflowing briefcase and slammed it shut. Damn. Jessie wished that she'd never met Captain Ben Adamanti. She wouldn't have had those days of ecstasy and excitement, but neither would she have the long line of empty days stretching out before her. Slamming the door behind her, Jessie stomped out of the classroom.

"Jessie."

Ben. His voice stirred all her nerve endings and filled her emptiness with spring. The birds were singing, the flowers were blooming and the joy of life frolicked like newborn bunnies in a field of clover. Jessie spun around.

One look at Ben's face was enough to put a screeching halt to her reverie. The ice in his eyes was like a series of No Trespassing signs, a high-voltage fence and a pack of vicious guard dogs all rolled into one. The message was clear. Stay back.

"Hello, Ben."

"How have you been?" he asked.

"Oh, just fine," she replied.

They paused, each to do a personal task. Jessie to check out the floor beneath her feet and Ben to scan the halls, now filled with departing students. Maybe he wanted to make sure that nobody stole any knowledge before they were ready for it.

"How is Maggie?"

"She's doing real good."

Ben just nodded. "I understand you're thinking of adopting her."

Her jaw muscles went tense for a long moment. Jessie wondered who had told him, Ethel or maybe one of his friends in the juvenile court system.

"I'm not just thinking about it," she said. "I've already put the wheels in motion to get it accomplished."

"Don't you think it's a little soon for that?"

Anger flooded her body, warming her cheeks and squeezing her lungs tight, making it difficult to breathe. "No, actually I think I'm late. About fourteen years late, but I don't see where my personal life is any of your business."

"You made a mistake, fourteen, fifteen years ago. That doesn't mean you have to spend the rest of your life paying for it."

Her anger was getting close to fury, and she could feel her stomach quiver. "Did you get a degree in psychology along with that degree in criminal justice, Captain Adamanti?"

A telltale red was growing in Ben's cheeks. "All I need is the common sense I was born with to see that this isn't right. You're on a crusade to make everything right. Save Maggie and ease your conscience. All in one fell swoop. You don't even know her, yet you're starting adoption proceedings. You aren't doing this for Maggie—you're doing it for yourself."

He was wrong, Jessie told herself, but she knew better than to try to explain. She'd had enough arguments with him to know that he didn't change his mind. He was as stubborn and thickheaded as they came. How could she ever have loved him? The angels must have been looking after her. They'd brought Maggie right in the nick of time.

"I really must be going," she said, trying to ease by him.

He reached out and grabbed her arm. "Don't you see how wrong this is? If it was a normal relationship, you wouldn't be so obsessed with Maggie."

"I'm not obsessed with her."

People turned to stare at them and then hurried off down the corridor, but Jessie didn't care. She was not going to be bullied by this stubborn fool of a man.

"Then why don't you have room in your life for anyone else but her?" Ben's voice was rising. "Ever since Maggie's come, you've squeezed everyone else out of your life."

"That's a lot of bull," she shouted. "You're just jealous of Maggie. If you weren't so possessive yourself, Maggie wouldn't have been a problem."

He stared at her a long time, the red in his face slowing turning to white. "If that's what you think of me, then our relationship is better off dead."

Then, turning on his heel, he stomped off down the hallway. Jessie was left shaking, her eyes burning. She almost ran out of the building to her car, not even thinking her keys might be locked inside. For once they weren't. Fumbling, she finally opened the door and rushed into her car, where she let the hot bitter tears flow.

"Is that your team over there?" Maggie asked as they got out of the car.

"Yes." Jessie got her mitt out of the trunk and stowed her purse in its place, carefully giving Maggie the car keys first. "We didn't have to come, you know. This isn't the way I would think most fourteen-year-olds would want to spend a Saturday afternoon."

"You guys lousy or something?"

"No, we're not lousy or anything," Jessie argued. "I just thought you might not be a softball fan."

Was it really that, or was it a reluctance to face Ben again? Marla had been raving all week about what a great player Ben was turning out to be, and bugging Jessie about the game on Saturday. Was she coming or not? Actually the answer had been no, except that Marla called to remind Jessie last night, and Maggie had taken the message. End of discussion. Jessie was going.

"Can I cheer real loud or will that embarrass you?"

"Only if you're calling attention to my mistakes," Jessie said.

The team spotted her when they got closer to the field and waved her over. Ben was in the crowd, though, and not one of the wavers. She knew she shouldn't have come.

"Hey, Jess is here."

"Hurry up, lazybones."

"Isn't that your cop boyfriend?" Maggie asked.

Jessie pushed her sunglasses up slightly, more to assure herself that her eyes were still safely covered than because they were slipping. "Yes, that's Ben. But he's not my boyfriend."

Maggie seemed not to hear the words. "Great, I can tell him that I have my first baby-sitting job tonight and that I should be paying off my shoes real soon."

"I'm sure he'll be glad to hear that."

They'd reached the field, and there was no putting off the inevitable. "Good luck," Maggie called, and hurried over to the bleachers.

Jessie put a brave smile on her face and joined her team.

"We thought you'd deserted us," someone said.

"Thought we were going to have to find a new catcher."

"Better get your gear on, the game's almost ready to start."

Getting on the shin guards and chest pad gave her something to do besides dwell on the fact that Ben hadn't said a word to her, hadn't even looked her way. It was for the best, she told herself. Sloppy, drawn-out endings were never her style. A clean, quick cut was better for all.

"Who's pitching?" she asked as she put her cap back on.

"I am."

Ben was standing off to the side, and for all his apparent unawareness of her, he had heard her question. His stance told her more than his voice about his feelings, though. There was stiffness in his shoulders that told her he was tense, and the way he was pounding the ball into his mitt said that he was anxious to get started, and probably anxious to leave. Well, so was she.

"Warm me up a little, then we can start," she said, then wished she could bite her words back.

There had to be other ways to say that wouldn't make her simple request sound like an invitation. But Ben seemed not to notice, and the catcher's mask hid her flushed cheeks. She hurried over to her place behind home plate.

Ben threw her a few pitches. Her returning throws were pretty weak at first, but by the last one she was doing better. She wasn't going to let him think that she was wasting away for lack of his company. He was the one who couldn't accept Maggie into his life.

The game started with the other team up to bat. Jessie concentrated. She missed a chance at a double play when her throw went wide, but other than that she had a reasonable inning. Nothing to hang her head over.

She did hang her head, literally, though, once it was their turn to bat. She stayed hunched over as she took off her pads, pretending to be engrossed while everyone else filed into the dugout. Avoiding everyone's eye, she could also avoid chatter and just slip in unnoticed to sit at the end of the bench.

Her plan didn't work. The end of the bench was taken, while a spot next to Ben had been left free. She went in and sat down. To be honest, he didn't look thrilled about the arrangement, either.

They watched in silence while Marla got on first base, then as Ron was walked. Ben shifted slightly, his arm brushing against hers. They both moved apart as if scorched, then seemed to realize how that must have looked.

"So how have you been?" Ben asked after a moment.

"Fine. And you?"

"Great. Just great."

Scintillating conversation. Then it was Ben's turn at bat, so she let him get by, his legs brushing hers, but she refused to let even the slightest touch affect her. She was strong enough and had pride enough to make it through the game without breaking down even the tiniest bit.

The game dragged on. She played all right—got on base three times and had a hand in a double play—but got no pleasure from any of it. Her eyes always seemed to find Ben, and her mind always seemed to think up things to say to him, even though she knew the words would never pass her lips. Make it through the game, her heart kept ordering her. Just make it through the game and you'll be fine.

By the last inning Jessie was worn out. Pretending her life was all happiness and sunshine was more exhausting than she expected. If the game wasn't over soon, she was going to give out. Even the sound of Maggie's voice in the stands, cheering her on each time the ball came near her, only brought her marginal pleasure. It was Ben and the ice in his eyes that set the tone for the afternoon.

Luckily they were ahead 5-4 with two outs and Jessie was mentally ticking off the seconds. But then the batter hit a double that got past Marla. Damn. Just let it be over.

The next batter hit a line drive into center field, but Ron lost it in the sun, catching it only after it bounced.

"Throw it home," she heard someone call out as she watched the runner race past third.

If this man scored, the game would be tied. If she got him out, the game would be over. She would either be here longer, watching Ben, loving him with her eyes and feeling the agony of his icy gaze, or she could go home and lick her wounds in private.

She took her place before home plate, blocking the runner's way as the ball came soaring to her. She reached up, caught it and held it out to tag the runner just as he dove into her. She went flying backward, landing hard on her back in the dust, and for a few moments felt the earth spin around her. Through her haze, she heard the umpire call the runner out. The game was over. She closed her eyes in blessed relief.

"Jess!"

Ben was leaning over her, then Marla and Ron and the others crowded around until she couldn't see Ben.

"Are you all right?"

"Jeez, what a jerk that guy was."

"Jessie, are you okay?" Maggie's voice came just as she was sitting up, and she looked around for the girl, finding Ben was moving to let Maggie in.

"Yeah, I'm okay." She tried to smile. "And I got the guy out."

"You sure did!"

With Maggie's help, Jessie got to her feet. Her left wrist was a little tender, but other than that she was all right. She caught sight of Ben's frowning face and amended her injury report. A tender wrist and a broken heart, but that was all. Satisfied that she was uninjured, the others moved away to gather their gear.

"Want to help me with these things?" Jessie asked Maggie as she tried to unclip the shin-guard straps. Her hands were shaking and unwilling to work right.

Maggie helped her with the shin guards, then tackled the chest pad. She was struggling with a clip on Jessie's back, when Jessie suddenly felt it go free. She turned to find that Ben had taken over.

"You shouldn't have gotten in his way," he snapped as he pulled the pad over her head and off. "You could have gotten hurt."

She was too close to him to think clearly. "I had the ball."

"You could have gotten hurt," he repeated.

"I won the game for us." All she wanted was a smile, a little hint of praise or pride. Something instead of that icy, forbidding gaze.

"That's not worth getting nearly creamed for." He handed her the pad and stomped off.

Maggie stood at her side, the shin guards clutched to her chest, as they both watched Ben gather his equipment from the dugout. "Jeez, I thought you were great," the girl said.

Jessie smiled in order to force back the tears that were threatening. "Thanks, honey."

"Hey, Jess," Marla called. "Coming for pizza?"

Ben stopped untying his shoe to look across at Jessie. She couldn't read his eyes, but knew he was listening.

"No," she said quickly. More time under Ben's disapproving gaze was more than she could take. "I think I've had enough excitement for one night."

Ben went back to changing his shoes and Jessie went back to breathing.

"Does everybody in the family know you're trying to adopt me?" Maggie asked.

The light turned red, giving Jessie time to flash Maggie a full smile. There was such a mixture of little-girl hope and fear of not being liked in her face that it almost broke Jessie's heart. This was what she would build her future happiness around, not the flightiness of a man's heart.

"There are a few distant cousins in England that we haven't been able to get a hold of," Jessie replied. "But outside of those, pretty much everybody knows."

Maggie let a silence fall, but it only lasted a few moments. "Is your father going to be at Denise's?"

Scowling in slight surprise, Jessie nodded. "Yes, Dad is going to be there. And my brother from Texas, who just came in this morning. Why?"

Maggie shrugged. "I don't know. I was just wondering how long I'd have to wait before I can call him Grandpa."

Jessie swallowed the lump in her throat and smiled. "Dad would be happy to have you call him Grandpa anytime you want."

With that bit of information, Maggie retreated into silence, staring out the window at the passing scene of farm fields and horses. She did that a lot. Taking data in spurts and then taking time to digest it. Jessie's own mind wandered as the traffic thinned.

Her family was welcoming Jessie with open arms. Denise had planned this party as soon as she had heard, even getting Danny and his family up here for it. Everything was turning out super where Maggie was concerned, and if Jessie's heart sometimes ached for Ben, well, it showed that she wasn't quite as strong as she thought she was.

Even that passing thought was enough to bring back the pain, but Jessie was getting used to it. It would come like a thief in the night, hitting her at all hours and no matter where she was and what she was doing. She wished that the two of them could have worked something out, but she should have known that it wouldn't be. She knew enough about love to know not to depend on it. Jessie swallowed hard and pulled up in front of Denise's house.

"Is that Grandpa?" Maggie asked, not quite able to hide the tremulous tone in her voice.

"Sure is." Jessie's father was standing on the porch, waving as Jessie pulled the car to a stop. He came down the steps toward them.

"Good afternoon, ladies."

"Hi, Dad," Jessie said as she exited the car.

"Hi," Maggie said with a nervous grin.

Jessie smiled. The poor kid. She so wanted to belong, but was still scared of rejection.

They all went inside, where both Jessie and Maggie were swallowed up in love and family. It was enough, Jessie told herself over and over again. She had her family and she had Maggie now; she didn't need Ben.

After some preliminary chatting, the whole group moved out into the backyard for badminton and croquet, then a raucous game of Frisbee before collapsing in lawn chairs with icy cold glasses of lemonade. The action was fine, kept

Jessie busy both in body and in mind, but lounging around seemed too dangerous.

She wondered what Ben was doing today. She'd managed to avoid him all week, though to be honest, it hadn't taken a great deal of effort. He hadn't called her or come to the office for anything. From her end, it had been a quiet week. No trips to the police station, not even any need to call there. And their last softball game had been rained out. There was talk of a team party, but so far nobody had done the legwork, so Jessie was hoping it would fall through. Though she no longer believed that avoiding Ben would keep him out of her thoughts.

"Did you always live around South Bend?" Denise asked Maggie idly, causing Jessie's eyes to open.

"No, I used to live near White Pigeon." One of Denise's kids had brought out a deck of cards and they were setting up a game of Go Fish.

"We lived in White Pigeon for a while," Danny said. "What was your family's name?"

"Evans," Maggie answered.

Denise and her father shook their heads—the name wasn't familiar to them. Jessie didn't know whether to be relieved or not. Someday she would tell Maggie about her baby, but she hadn't decided when. Did that mean keeping it from the family, too?

The card game started. Maggie, being the oldest, was trying to keep everyone in line, but soon the little group of kids dissolved into laughter and giggles. It was good to hear laughter again. That was something Ben had brought into her life, and it was hard to find without him.

"When's your birthday, Maggie?" one of Denise's kids asked. "Mine is December 23 and that's really yucky."

"June 3, I guess. I was adopted and got a new name so maybe I got a new birthday, too," Maggie said. "Hey, you guys know how to play gin rummy?"

Denise turned to look at Jessie, question marks flashing in her eyes.

"Time to start dinner," Denise announced suddenly, and got to her feet. "Jess, can you give me a hand?"

Jessie knew exactly what Denise really wanted and followed her into the house.

"Jessie?"

She took a deep breath. "I don't know for sure," Jessie said. "But deep in my heart I'm . . . I'm sure she's the little girl I gave up."

"Oh, my God, Jessie." Denise hugged her tight, tears flowing down her cheeks. "We got her back. Back with her family where she belongs."

"Nobody stole her, Denise. None of us could care for her."

"I know, I know," Denise said. She wiped at her eyes with the back of her hands. "It's just that it's so wonderful. Our whole family is back together again."

The tears and joy in Denise's eyes were genuine, yet they bothered Jessie. What if Maggie wasn't her child? Would Denise accept her just as well, or would there always be a wall making Maggie different?

Denise took Jessie's hand and pulled her over to the table. "Now, what about your boyfriend?" she asked. "How's he taking this?"

Jessie just shrugged. "He's not. We broke up."

Denise frowned. "Just like Randy. Ducks out when you need him."

"No, he wasn't like Randy at all," Jessie protested. Ben wasn't; the comparison was unfair. "Ben was kind and thoughtful and loving."

"And gone," Denise noted dryly. She got up and opened a beer for each of them.

Jessie held hers, the can's chill wetting her hand. ''But it was for different reasons. Ben's mother abandoned him when he was a baby, and in his mind, I did the same thing.''

''He said that?''

Jessie shrugged, trying to remember just how things went. ''Well, I didn't exactly stay around long enough to let him.''

Denise sipped at her beer. ''You assumed he wouldn't stay around and broke up with him before he could leave.''

Did she do the breaking up, though? Jessie frowned as she tried to remember every conversation she'd had with Ben lately. All she knew was that she had been so afraid he would reject her that she was careful not to give him the chance. Why? A sudden chill took hold of her heart. Was Denise right? Had she taken away his chance to accept her, too?

The noises from outside changed, and Denise went to the door to peer out. The next thing Jessie knew, Denise was flying out the door, yelling her son's name.

''Kyle, you get down from that tree this minute. Just what do you think you're doing?''

Jessie got to the screen door in time to see a remorseful five-year-old being lifted from a low branch of an apple tree.

''I was just showing Maggie how good I can climb,'' the little boy said.

''He said you let him climb the tree,'' Maggie said.

Denise just grimaced. ''Men. Half of what they do is to show off, the other half is to hide their wounded pride.'' She turned toward her husband. ''Larry, get the kids into something safe while Jess and I fix dinner, will you?''

Was Ben keeping his distance because of wounded pride? Jessie felt bombarded with worries. This pleasant family picnic was opening a whole new set of questions, ones that had no easy answers, either.

* * *

"How come Denise got so mad at Kyle?" Maggie asked as they drove home through the darkness.

"Because she loves him, and when you love someone, you get angry when they do something foolish. It's like they aren't cherishing themselves the way you cherish them."

"Oh." Maggie let the silence settle around them for a moment. "Like when your cop boyfriend got mad at you at the softball game?"

Jessie felt the stars stand still to listen. She took a deep breath, then shook her head. "Not exactly. And he's not my boyfriend anymore."

"When did you break up?"

"Oh, about—" Jessie stopped. She and Ben had broken up right before Maggie moved in. That wasn't something she wanted to lay on the child.

"You broke up when I moved in, didn't you?"

Jessie bit at her lip a moment. Damn.

"Doesn't he like me?" Maggie asked.

"Honey, honey." Jessie put her free arm around Maggie's shoulders. "You have nothing to do with it. We're just two adults who made a mutual decision."

"My mom always said there was no such thing as a mutual decision. She said one person always gives in because he thinks it's what the other person wants."

That coincided a little too closely to Denise's philosophy for comfort, but Jessie was through with philosophy. Ben could have called her if he'd wanted their relationship to continue. Period. End of discussion.

"Well, this was one of those rare, real mutual decisions," Jessie said.

Luckily they were just about home, so the conversation could end. Unfortunately her mind kept playing it over and over again even without Maggie's help. Had Jessie leapt to conclusions because she was so afraid? Had she pushed Ben away because of her fear he would leave? It didn't sound sensible; it didn't sound sane. But when had love ever been sensible or sane?

Maggie went to bed, and so did Captain Kidd, but Jessie stayed up trying to read. When her witnesses were all gone, she gave up the pretense and went to stare out the window. Had she used Maggie as an excuse to ease Ben out of her life? Suddenly she couldn't remember anything but his hurt and his pain.

It was almost midnight, but she couldn't wait any longer. Picking up the phone, she dialed his home number. His answering machine came on.

"Ben, it's me. Jessie. Call me when you get home. Whatever time it is."

There was nothing else to say, not to an answering machine, but she was reluctant to hang up. It was like bridging the connection to him. Captain Kidd came out of her bedroom to stare at her, drawn no doubt by the sound of her voice. She felt silly holding the receiver under his unblinking gaze and hung up.

"Call soon, Ben," she whispered to the night. Call soon.

Eleven

Ben finished the report, then tossed it into the wrong basket on his desk. He grabbed for it impatiently and succeeded in knocking over the whole basket. Papers spilled all over the floor. Damn and double damn.

That message from Jessie on his answering machine last night had thrown him. He had no intention of returning her call—he wasn't into masochism—but he couldn't get it out of his mind, either. Why couldn't she just leave him alone? He walked around his desk and started picking up his papers.

A knock sounded at his door, then it opened. "Captain Adamanti?"

Ben looked up from the floor. It was Maggie. "What can I do for you?"

She bent down, reaching for a sheaf of papers under his desk and handing it to him. "You throwing stuff around, too? Jeez, you guys are in bad shape."

"I knocked something over," Ben said carefully as he stood up. "I was not throwing stuff around."

"Uh-huh." Maggie sat down in front of his desk. "Sure, and Jessie's not sleeping at night because she's just not ever tired anymore."

The mention of Jessie's name was enough to send his eyes to his appointment calendar. "Is there something I can do for you? I have a rather busy morning." Right, he had only three more hours to prepare for taking his books back to the library.

Maggie crossed her legs, resting her right foot on her left knee so that she could fiddle with the laces. "I was just curious about you and Jessie," the girl said. "You know, like how come you broke up and stuff like that."

Just what he needed, a teenage Dear Abby. "You figure that's any of your business?" he snapped.

But Maggie's look turned belligerent. "It is if you dumped her because of me."

He heard the pain behind her toughness and sighed. Everybody was hurting in this mess. "What makes you think I did? Did Jessie say so?"

Maggie shook her head. "She said it was a mutual decision."

"So why are you doubting her?"

"Because she's hurting and you're throwing stuff around. It doesn't sound like anybody's happy. I don't want it to be because of me."

Ben looked over at the girl. Her eyes were dark and troubled. "It's not," he finally said reassuringly. "We just had some basic disagreements. It would have happened whether you came along or not."

"Oh."

Ben didn't want to be rude, but neither did he want to spend his morning discussing Jessie. "So how's everything else going? You still helping out at the youth center?"

"Yeah, and I've got about a third of my shoes paid for." She frowned down at her feet. "I guess that's maybe the laces, the soles and one tongue."

Ben got to his feet, laying a hand on the girl's shoulder. "I'm glad things are working out for you. Jessie's determined that they do."

Maggie nodded and got to her feet. "Jessie doesn't know that I came. She'd probably skin me alive if she did."

"I won't tell her," Ben promised. He doubted there would be a chance to.

Once Maggie was gone, he tried to get back to work, to concentrate on an article in a law enforcement periodical, but his mind wouldn't cooperate. He saw Jessie's laughing eyes and heard the soft tones of her voice that played havoc with his sanity. He remembered her sitting on the edge of his desk, that day after they'd been to the beach, and the silky heat of her skin.

He jumped to his feet. He had to get out of here. She was haunting this place.

The phone seemed to be frowning at her, its silence mocking. Jessie tried turning so that she couldn't see the stupid thing, but could still feel its presence. This was crazy, she finally decided. She was an adult. She was not intimidated by a telephone, no matter how silent it was.

Why didn't Ben call? Maybe he hadn't listened to his machine when he'd got in last night. It seemed the height of immaturity to sit here waiting for the phone to ring. She grabbed up the receiver and dialed Ben's office, only to learn he was out for the rest of the day.

Now what? Jessie hung up the phone slowly. She was tired of this waiting, tired of the hope building in her heart when it might just be setting her up for an even bigger fall. She had to get things settled tonight.

After calling his office back and being assured he had no meetings scheduled for that evening, Jessie called Denise and arranged for her to take Maggie for the night. Then Jessie tried to work the rest of the day. It was hard and she didn't accomplish much, but the clock finally inched forward to quitting time.

She'd start off by telling Ben that she'd been afraid, she planned as she left the office. She'd tell him that because his mother had abandoned him, she'd been afraid he would think she'd done the same thing. She'd tell him that because she hadn't been able to risk his rejection, she did the rejecting.

What he'd say, she had no idea. He might tell her to take a flying leap, but he might just be missing her as much as she was missing him. She pulled her car up in front of his house.

The sky was clouding over, and the air had a chill to it that was unusual for August. She hoped it wasn't an omen and marched up to his front door. Smile, she ordered herself. Present a positive image, and maybe it will come true.

She knocked at his door and rang the bell. Neither produced an answer. Shoot. She must have beaten him home. She walked around back and peered into his garage. Empty. All right, so she would just wait. She'd get a book from the car and read while she waited for Ben to come home.

Jessie walked back to her car, then stopped. The keys were inside. Of all the lamebrained things to do!

The clouds were getting darker and more ominous. Rats, rats, rats. The first few drops came spattering down, and Jessie hurried around the back of the house. No umbrellas left outside for irresponsible visitors, no new porch roofs to hide under. Nothing but a picnic table.

The rain was starting to come down in earnest, and Jessie dived under the table. This was so silly.

She hugged her legs to her, laying her face against her knees. She had blown her last chance at happiness, and this was the gods' way of telling her. Ben was probably out of town for the rest of the year, and she would sit here all night. Or else he would come home, find her here and arrest her for trespassing.

The rain was coming down in sheets, splashing onto the concrete patio and dripping down between the boards of the table and onto her. What parts of her the splashing and dripping didn't reach, the water running across the patio did. She hugged her knees tighter, trying to make herself smaller. It didn't work. Her leather pumps were drenched, her cotton skirt was soaking up water like a sponge and her silk blouse put wet-T-shirt contests to shame.

Jessie stared at her watch as she huddled under the table. How long should she wait? She was about a ten-minute walk from the nearest public building—a hospital, of all places. How fitting. She could walk over and check herself in for a broken heart, insanity and pneumonia.

Twenty minutes, she suddenly decided. That's how long she would sit here. But when her watch reached eighteen minutes, thirty-seven seconds, she noticed a pair of leather shoes approaching her. Then Ben bent over to peer under the table. His frown was the first thing that registered.

"What the hell are you doing?"

"Trying to stay dry." She let him help out, her joints stiff from the dampness.

"It didn't work."

"No, it didn't." Her hair was plastered to her cheeks, so that it matched her blouse and skirt. Her shoes squished as she walked.

Ben led her over to his back door and ushered her inside. The air-conditioned air felt as though it came straight from the Arctic. She started shivering and wrapped her arms around her chest. Ben gave her a look, but said nothing as he closed the door, then led her through the living room and into the bedroom.

"Your keys in the car?" he asked as he pulled a robe from his closet.

She nodded, her teeth chattering too much to speak. She tried to unbutton her blouse, but her fingers didn't want to work.

"I guessed as much." He came over and began to unbutton the blouse for her. His eyes reflected his irritation with her, not a spark of desire weakening it. "Sometimes I think you need a keeper."

"Someone who can make eggs Benedict?"

He frowned and stripped off her blouse, wrapping his robe around her shoulders. "Can you manage the skirt?"

She nodded, but her fingers weren't paying attention. They wouldn't work there, either. With a sigh Ben unbuttoned the waistband and unzipped the skirt. It fell to the floor around her ankles. As he pulled the robe more tightly about her, she saw a white line of tension around his mouth that hadn't been there before.

"Come on, I'll make you some tea," he said, and hurried toward the kitchen without waiting to see if she was following.

His robe was almost as good as his arms. Warm, with his own scent clinging to it. Jessie took heart that he hadn't thrown her out, and went after him.

"I came to apologize," she said as she entered the kitchen.

He glanced up from the stove, but his eyes were in shadow.

She came closer and leaned against the sink cabinet. "I'm not really good when it comes to relationships and communicating."

Ben just got two mugs out of a cabinet over the stove and placed a tea bag in each. "Oh, I don't know. You seemed to talk pretty well the other night."

"I said all the wrong things."

She couldn't bear to watch his back turned toward her so that she could build no hope from the look in his eyes. He wasn't making this any easier for her. She tied and untied the belt of the robe, watching how the soft fabric curled around itself.

"When I got pregnant, I didn't know what to do. I was afraid to tell my dad, and somehow thought Randy was going to make everything all right. He ran. I mean, he actually left town. I didn't see him again. I guess his parents were so afraid that I was going to force him to marry me that they sent him away. But that was the last thing I wanted. I just wanted some support."

A faint whistle signaled that the water was boiling. A few seconds later Ben put her steaming mug near her arm.

"I guess I was pretty numb the whole time I was pregnant. Nothing seemed to penetrate my fog, but once I had the baby and gave her up, it seemed like my whole world had fallen apart. All I did was cry."

"To be expected, I would guess."

His voice was softer, less angry, but her vision was blurred with tears and she couldn't risk a glance in his direction. "Everything that meant love was gone. Randy. The baby. Even my mother. I vowed I would never get close to anyone else again. I wasn't going to let myself get hurt like that again."

She picked up her cup, wrapping her hands around it to pull the warmth through the sides. She watched the steam rising, rather than Ben.

"I was doing pretty good until I met you," she went on. "Then everything started to change. I told myself I was still in control, but when Maggie came into my life, I panicked. I was so afraid that history was going to repeat itself, that when I told you the truth, you would leave. So rather than finding out where we stood, I filled my life with her and shoved you out."

She forced herself to look up then, though her eyes were swimming with tears and Ben was just a blur across the kitchen from her. "So anyway, that's why I'm here. To ask you where we stand."

This was where he was supposed to take her in his arms and tell her he'd missed her so, that he loved her, too. But neither of them moved. Was the distance across the kitchen too far to cross? Was the chasm she'd furrowed too deep?

"I was away a few days last week," Ben said.

His voice was carefully neutral. Jessie would have preferred anger to indifference. Her heart cracked a bit more, but she kept her chin up. Whether he loved her or not, she would let him know all the things he'd helped her see.

"Oh?"

"Went up to Michigan." He sipped at his tea, then put the cup down. "I looked up Maggie's adoption records. I wanted to find out for you whether or not she was your child."

"Why?"

"Because you were hurting so. You were so racked with guilt, I couldn't bear it. I thought maybe if you learned the truth about Maggie's parents—learned whether you had really failed her or not—you could let the past go."

Jessie blinked the wetness from her eyes so that she could see. "The records are sealed."

He shrugged. "I know some people up there."

Silence fell over the room like a heavy, wet blanket of snow. She finally turned to stare out the window at the rain-streaked view of the backyard. A million different thoughts and emotions raced through her heart. In her mind she saw her baby, all red and wrinkled and crying. Then she saw Maggie's scared eyes when they'd gone to the police station that night lifetimes ago, and the girl's laughing eyes this morning over breakfast. Jessie turned.

"I know Maggie's mine," she said simply. "She became mine a few weeks ago when my foster parent application was approved, and she'll become more mine when the adoption goes through."

Ben just watched her. "Don't you want to know if she's the child you gave up?"

Jessie shrugged. "It doesn't matter." She took a deep breath. "You were right. I was trying to make up for the past fourteen years, but I can't. I don't have to. I did what was best for everybody back then. It wasn't my fault some of it turned out badly. Yesterday at Denise's I began to see that who Maggie is now is what counts now, not who she was fourteen years ago."

"Oh, Jess." His words were a sigh, softer than a whisper, but he had found a way to bridge the gap across the room and took her in his arms. "Welcome home."

Jessie lay against his chest, breathing in his closeness and feeling alive for the first time in ages. "I'm so sorry for the way I handled everything," she said. "I don't handle love very well."

His hand stroked her wet hair, pushing it back from her forehead. "Your love for Maggie?"

She took a deep breath, then shook her head. "No, for you. I know it wasn't what we had planned, but I fell in love with you. If I hadn't cared so much, I probably wouldn't have pushed you out of my life."

Ben's arms tightened around her. "I think there's logic in there somewhere," he teased. "Or maybe it's just that I was in the same boat, so I understand."

She pushed back slightly so she could look up into his eyes. "Ben?"

"I love you, too," he said softly. "It wasn't what I was looking for, either, but it happened. The night you told me about your baby was the night I realized it. I should have told you, tried to make you see that you had room for both Maggie and me in your life, but I was afraid to believe that you were different than the other women I've known. And it seemed for a time that I didn't know you at all. It was only a moment ago, when you said you didn't care if Maggie was your baby, that I realized the woman who had enough love for all the kids in trouble also had room in her heart for me."

She gazed up at him and saw her own love shining back at her. "Oh, Ben."

His lips came down on hers in a kiss that told her better than any words just how much he cared. All her fears had been for nothing. She had brought winter into her life when it still should have been spring.

Ben's touch ignited her heart, and her body quivered with relief and joy. His hands pulled her close, sliding under the robe and warming her skin with desire. She moved to him, her heart pounding. She had never believed such happiness could be hers.

"I've been so miserable without you," Ben whispered, his lips leaving hers to touch her forehead, then her hair. "How can two seemingly smart people be so stupid?"

She didn't bother to answer; she was too busy touching him, loving the feel of their closeness. All the misery of the past few weeks had to be wiped away and in his arms was the place to do it. The heat of their passion was the way back to happiness.

Ben suddenly picked her up in his arms and carried her back to the bedroom. With the rain pounding a rhythm on the roof and the evening shadows closing in on them, they lay together on his bed. His hands touched her, stroked every inch of her, while her caress promised she would always be there for him.

Their hands, lips and hearts spoke of hunger and passion, but also of devotion and love. The hurts were erased and forgotten, and sunshine for all the tomorrows was promised. The love they shared was sweeter than it had ever been, and afterward, they lay in each other's arms, feeling blessed.

"Tell me something," Ben murmured into her hair. "Is Captain Kidd very adaptable?"

It wasn't what she expected to discuss in the afterglow of lovemaking and frowned at him. "No."

Ben did not seem to realize how silly this topic was. He looked serious. "So how do we convince him to move in here?"

Jessie found a slow smile creeping into her heart. "In here?"

"Well, I doubt that you want to keep paying rent on the apartment just for him." He gazed down at her, his eyes alight with love and hope. "And since once we get married, you and Maggie will be living here with me, I was worried about Captain Kidd."

"Oh, are we getting married?"

Ben brushed her lips with his. "Yes. You need somebody to keep track of your car keys on a permanent basis."

"True."

He kissed her again, slower, sweeter. "And kids should grow up in a house, not an apartment, so that means you've got to move in here and give up your apartment."

"True again." She felt his warmth surround her, his love making her safe.

"So how do we convince the Captain that he's going to be happy here?"

Jessie snuggled up closer to Ben. "Promise him all the windowsills in the house and eggs Benedict for breakfast." She closed her eyes and let her happiness chase away any lingering shadows forever. Fairy tales really did come true.

* * * * *